A Most Unpleasant Wedding

A Most Unpleasant Wedding

Judith Alguire

EDITIONS

Cover design by Doowah Design.
Photo of Judith Alguire by Taylor Studios, Kingston.

This book was printed on Ancient Forest Friendly paper.
Printed and bound in Canada by Hignell Printing Inc.

We acknowledge the support of the Canada Council for the Arts and the
Manitoba Arts Council for our publishing program.

Library and Archives Canada Cataloguing in Publication

Alguire, Judith
          A most unpleasant wedding / Judith Alguire.

(A Rudley mystery ; 3)
Issued also in electronic formats.
ISBN 978-1-897109-99-1

          I. Title. II. Series: Alguire, Judith. Rudley mystery ; 3.

PS8551.L477M68 2012   C813'.54   C2012-906320-7

Signature Editions
P.O. Box 206, RPO Corydon, Winnipeg, Manitoba, R3M 3S7
www.signature-editions.com

To my great-niece Audrey

Chapter One

Waves carrying the subdued sheen of late afternoon licked the dock at the Pleasant Inn, rocking the red canoe tied up alongside. June. Perfect day. Seventy-two degrees with a light breeze that rustled the leaves of the oaks and mixed and diffused the fragrances of pine resin, wild rose, and cedar. The motorboat dashing about in the distance was too remote to destroy the ambiance, its wake too removed to disturb the only other boat on the water. Norman Phipps-Walker lay stretched out in his rowboat, thirty yards off the dock, dozing against his pillow. His fishing line drifted on the swell.

Lloyd Brawly, maintenance man for the Pleasant, worked in the flower bed at the bottom of the lawn, periodically glancing toward the rowboat. He had promised Geraldine Phipps-Walker he would keep an eye on Norman while she searched the back lawn for the cedar waxwing whose sharp *twee-twee* had roused her from the veranda.

The grounds were quiet, but life was beginning to stir in the rooms at the main inn and in the scattered cottages. From the High Birches to the Pines, from the Sycamore to the Oaks, guests woke from their afternoon naps and began to prepare for dinner.

Walter Sawchuck made an unproductive visit to the bathroom, then helped his wife, Doreen, over the edge of the bed. Walter had prostate trouble but had managed to dodge surgery for several years. Doreen had arthritis, and although she took a while to get going, managed to function with an assortment of canes and staffs, one of them an evil, metal-tipped walking stick from a Bavarian jaunt. The Sawchucks were proud natives of Rochester, New York. They wore identical Lands' End leisure wear. They had been coming to the Pleasant since Trigger was a colt and thought no other place could compare. Here they were accorded the respect they thought due a retired Kodak executive and his wife. Trevor and Margaret Rudley and staff catered to their every need. In spite of the Pleasant's history of unfortunate events, the Sawchucks, for whatever misguided reason, felt entirely safe at the inn.

James Bole at the Sycamore, a secluded cottage surrounded by pines, put the finishing touches on his finger puppets before dressing for dinner. Mr. Bole had received a liberal arts education at the University of Toronto and had undertaken considerable independent study in the sciences and languages. He was independently wealthy and had never worked a day in his life, but had travelled the world in search of enlightenment. He spoke several languages but was especially fond of the classics. Unfortunately, the only people at the Pleasant who could speak a word of Latin were the Benson sisters, the elderly trio who occupied the Elm Pavilion, a large circular structure with a wraparound veranda to the left of the Pleasant. Since much of their vocabulary came from Caesar's *Commentaries on the Gallic Wars*, the content of their conversations was limited. Mr. Bole took a moment to examine the puppets for his latest finger-puppet show: *Waiting for Godot.*

Jack Arnold picked up his hat, paused, put his hat down, and poured two fingers of Glenlivet. The once-successful contractor had chosen the Pleasant by throwing a fistful of brochures into the air. The one that landed closest to him was the winner. He knew he should have been pleased with his selection — the place was as pretty as any place he had visited, the food was superb — the little Frenchman, Gregoire, knew how to cook. He took a long drink. Not much action though. Most of the places he visited had at least a couple of presentable, available women. The only unattached women here were the three old dolls in the Elm Pavilion, a waitress who looked like jailbait, and a housekeeper named Tiffany who, he suspected, would skewer him with her broom if he made a false move. So tonight he would do what he had done the last couple of nights — have dinner at the inn, then go to the hotel in town and take his chances. He would run his Visa card to the maximum for this vacation, but he needed the break. When he got back home, he'd turn things around. All he needed was one good contract. He paused, stared at his whisky. It'd been a while since he'd had a good contract. He drained his glass and poured another drink.

Rico Carty pulled on his shoes and ran a hand over his close-cropped hair. At twenty-two, he was short and wiry with bronzed skin that spoke of his Guatemalan heritage. He was a bit in awe of the Pleasant. He hadn't expected it to be so nice. He was embarrassed he had nothing in his wardrobe but T-shirts and jeans. A lot of the guests dressed casually, but he could tell their clothes were expensive. Most of the people were older too. So far, everyone had treated him with respect. He appreciated that. But he didn't know how things were going to work out and felt apprehensive. He planned to slip up to the inn for dinner and do what he had done at lunch — order a lot of food and ask for a doggy bag. Tim, the elegant waiter who looked like a young Paul Newman, hadn't batted an eye at his request and had even offered extra rolls and dessert. He took a deep breath and told himself everything would be fine.

Tee and Bonnie Lawrence dressed for dinner. He chose a lightweight tan suit with a silk shirt and tie. She wore a dress suitable for evening, pumps, and a scarf that matched his tie. The insignia on his tie clasp matched the insignia on her earrings. His watch matched hers. Bonnie had commissioned the watches for their tenth anniversary and had had them inscribed — *Tee and Bonnie forever*. The Lawrences were a Natalie Wood/Robert Wagner sort of couple, too cute to project the mystique of a Bogart and Bacall. Indeed, people often referred to them as *that cute little couple*.

The Lawrences had ambitions. Tee came from a family of political kingmakers. Those in the know assumed Tee would run for a seat in Parliament. He had paid his dues — president of the Young Conservatives, president of his local riding — and expected to be nominated unchallenged. Bonnie, his backers believed, would be the perfect political wife: gifted with social graces without coming across as particularly intelligent — which she was not — pretty without being glamorous. She had that precious combination of devotion and vulnerability that played well with their base, men and women alike. Tee's team licked their chops as they imagined the picture on the brochures. Tee and Bonnie were irresistible.

Miss Pearl Dutton leaned into the mirror to refresh her lipstick — Sweet Temptress — and got back a blurry image. She could see cataract surgery in her future. But not right now. She could see well enough to get around and found her inferior vision an asset in assessing suitable men of her age. She thought, so far, Rudley, her nephew-in-law and co-proprietor of the Pleasant, had done a poor job of booking appropriate men this season. His oversight didn't bother her as much as it might have. She had been seeing Nick Anderson from town quite regularly since his hip surgery, and if Nick's attentions faltered, there was always the gentleman across the bay. She paused, squinted. Smiled. There were definitely times when myopia could be a plus.

Miss Elizabeth Miller, the young librarian from Toronto, and her fiancé, Mr. Edward Simpson, also of Toronto, via London, England, had been coming to the Pleasant three years running and had decided, much to the pleasure and excitement of the staff and regular guests, to hold their wedding ceremony here. Edward was a handsome young man; Elizabeth was a spirited young woman. The older guests commented on how much she reminded them of Eleanor Roosevelt, or at least a combination of Eleanor and Anne of Green Gables. No one considered her beautiful except Edward. Everyone agreed she was spunky. As bright as a new penny, the Benson sisters liked to say. Most believed Miss Miller had missed her true calling by choosing to be a librarian and freelance writer: she would have made a great detective and an incomparable spy. Miss Miller was perspicacious; she was audacious. And right now, she was aiming the motorboat toward the Pleasant at full throttle while Simpson held onto his hat and made the occasional cautionary remark about the probability of running the boat into the dock, or Norman, or Lloyd, depending on the angle of approach. Miss Miller ignored his warnings because Miss Miller was fearless and had complete faith in her abilities. Simpson was not fearless, but his good breeding prevented him from making a fuss. Miss Miller roared toward the dock, then at the last moment, turned sharply, cut the engines, and drifted neatly to a mooring ring.

Simpson allowed the blood to return to his head, then cleared his throat and said, "Well done, Elizabeth."

She smiled. "Thank you, Edward."

Dinner would be served imminently. A number of the guests had gathered on the veranda, waiting for the doors to open. Tim kept them at bay with trays of canapés and aperitifs. Among those gathered were Bonnie and Tee Lawrence, Mr. Bole, Aunt Pearl Dutton, Geraldine and Norman Phipps-Walker, and Doreen and Walter Sawchuck. Jack Arnold drifted up from his cabin, not because of any shortage of libation in his own cabinet, but because he was hoping a new guest might have arrived, someone female, young, and, if not young, at least presentable.

Tim deposited a tray of canapés on each table, then began to take orders for drinks.

Rico Carty came up the steps, hesitated.

"Please join us," said Tim. "We have some scrumptious snacks, and I'm taking drink orders."

"Sit here," said Geraldine, patting the chair beside her.

Miss Miller and Mr. Simpson joined the group.

"How was your trip?" Tim asked. "Did you like the new boat?"

Miss Miller beamed. "Wonderful. Quick. Nimble. Responsive."

"I trust you put it through its paces," said Mr. Bole. "I saw your landing on my way up."

Simpson winced. "It was rather spectacular." He turned to Rico. "I'm sorry. I don't believe we've met. Edward Simpson from Toronto, and"—he turned to Miss Miller—"Elizabeth Miller, also from Toronto." He offered his hand.

"Rico Carty from Ottawa."

Arnold interrupted the pleasantries. "Waiter, Glenlivet, straight."

"Of course." Tim turned to Rico. "What would you like?"

"Do you have lemonade?"

"Pink or regular?"

"Pink, if you have it."

Jack Arnold hooted. Rico blushed.

"I'll have a Mill Street Lager, please," said Miss Miller, giving Arnold a steely look.

"Bass for me, Tim, thank you," said Simpson.

Tim took the rest of the orders. Simpson turned to Carty. "Are you planning to do some fishing, Mr. Carty?"

"A little. Maybe some canoeing. Mostly I'm just here to relax."

"You've come to the right place," said Mr. Bole. "I can't think of a more idyllic place than the Pleasant."

Tim returned with the drinks just as Arnold broke into a paroxysm of sneezing. Bonnie Lawrence looked at him in horror as he grabbed a serviette and blew his nose, ending with a decisive honk.

"Some damned weed around here," said Arnold. He took a package of Benadryl from his pocket, cracked the cellophane wrapper, and popped two capsules from the blister pack. He washed the pills down with the whisky.

"I don't think you should do that," Carty blurted out.

"Do what?"

"Mix Benadryl with alcohol."

Arnold stared at him. "Are you a doctor or something?"

"I've taken pharmacy courses. Besides, it says that on the box."

Arnold gave him a disdainful look. "Maybe the box is referring to guys who drink pink lemonade."

Carty blushed.

"I think Mr. Carty was trying to be helpful," said Miss Miller. "Perhaps he thought it would be unfortunate if you keeled over on the veranda so close to dinner."

Arnold sneered at her.

Bonnie Lawrence broke in. "Miss Miller, Mr. Simpson, let me take the opportunity to congratulate you on your upcoming wedding."

Tee nodded, lifted his glass.

"Thank you."

"I hear the weather should be perfect."

"We're prepared for anything," Miss Miller said. "If it rains we'll just pull on our slickers."

"Quite," said Simpson. "Should be jolly good fun."

"It's nice to see a couple so relaxed about their wedding," said Tee.

"We're just hoping everyone enjoys the day," said Simpson. "I think people remember a wedding more fondly if it's not overly formal."

Arnold guffawed. "Believe me, Simpson, by the time it's over, they'll have turned it into a three-ring circus. My ex-wife and her mother spent months worrying about the cocktail napkins clashing with the flower girl's dress, or the groom's mother's shoes, or whatever. You'd be smarter to use the money to put a down payment on a house."

Bonnie broke in. "There's nothing contradictory about a wedding being a pleasant experience while adhering to a well-thought-out theme." She looked to Miss Miller for support.

Miss Miller sampled her beer before responding. "We don't have a theme. We thought we'd just go with the flow."

After a long pause, Bonnie returned to what she assumed would be safe territory. "Will the wedding be on the lawn?"

"We haven't decided yet," said Miss Miller.

"Perhaps on the rise," said Simpson.

"Or in the swamp by the dock," said Miss Miller.

"She means on the dock by the swamp," said Simpson.

Bonnie clutched at this straw. "The idea of the dock has potential. I've seen some lovely weddings using the water as a backdrop. After, the bride tosses the bouquet onto the waves. A beautiful ending to the ceremony, I think, with its connotations of eternal love."

Tee sighed. "You should do commercials for destination weddings, Bonnie." He gave Miss Miller an apologetic smile. "Weddings are one of Bonnie's obsessions."

Bonnie shrank in her chair. "I just thought I could offer some ideas, dear."

"That's very kind of you," Simpson said before Miss Miller could open her mouth.

Miss Miller forced a smile. "Of course, I'd be grateful for your help, Mrs. Lawrence."

Bonnie brightened. "Please, it's Tee and Bonnie."

"Then, Edward and Elizabeth."

The dinner bell rang. To reinforce the invitation, Tim appeared in the doorway. "Dinner is served."

Tee and Bonnie excused themselves. Arnold hauled himself up and left. Rico stared at the plate of canapés.

"Finish those, young man," said Aunt Pearl. "You've got plenty of time."

"Elizabeth," said Simpson, "I believe you came perilously close to impudence."

She tossed her head. "I'm sorry, Edward. There's something about the Lawrences that brings out my sassy side."

Mr. Bole nodded. "I expect you find them a bit…ordinary."

"I hate the idea of coordinated match covers and serviettes."

Mr. Bole chuckled. "You could probably skip the matches altogether, unless you're planning to set fire to the place."

"Bite your tongue," said Aunt Pearl. "You know how things happen around here." She leaned toward Rico. "I don't want to alarm you, dear, but things happen around here."

He swallowed a canapé. "Things?"

"We've had the odd mishap," said Mr. Bole, "which is why Miss Dutton objected to my facetious remark."

Rico nodded. He wrapped the remainder of the canapés in his serviette. "Sorry. Excuse me."

"Of course." Pearl watched Carty disappear into the lobby. "Lovely young man." She turned to Miss Miller. "I know what you mean about the Lawrences. I'm sure they're just fine, but that Ken and Barbie act is a bit much."

"They have matching accessories," said Miss Miller.

"Precious," said Aunt Pearl.

Mr. Bole nodded. "Rather conventional couple. I imagine Mrs. Lawrence's taste in weddings tends toward the gaudy. In my opinion, the quirky ones are the most fun. I once attended a wedding on the Nile. The couple — they were Egyptologists — and the entire wedding party dressed as the court of King Tut."

Aunt Pearl gave him a bleary look over her martini. "Ever think of tying the knot, James?"

He hesitated. "There was a young woman at the University of Toronto when I was a graduate student." He thought for a moment. "And a young lady I met later — music tour of Europe — and a young woman I met while studying Thomson's gazelle in Tanganyika, as it was called then." He paused. "I'm not trying to impress you as a Casanova by any means. Just to say I've met many interesting women through the years, all of whom would have made a man consider matrimony."

Aunt Pearl smirked. "Well, as they say, it's the thought that counts."

Mr. Bole finished his gin and tonic. "Of course, men are more apt to be marriageable when we're young. We tend to get set in our ways as we get older." He put his glass down. "Ladies and gentlemen, if you'll excuse me, my mouth is watering for Gregoire's filet mignon."

Aunt Pearl turned to her Drambuie chaser. "James Bole is afraid a woman might come between him and his finger puppets."

Miss Miller tilted her head. "Aunt Pearl, do you have designs on Mr. Bole?"

She waved this off. "Hell, no. I've known James Bole for years. He's like a brother to me. Besides being a lousy dancer, he can't play poker, and has no sense of humour to speak of. I can't imagine being that desperate."

Trevor and Margaret Rudley, proprietors of the Pleasant Inn, were at the front desk as the guests drifted in for dinner. Albert, their large, hairy dog, lay on the rug in the centre of the lobby, rolling over periodically to trip the uninitiated.

"Mrs. Sawchuck," Rudley said as she hobbled past the desk, "I wanted you to know that I've apprehended the centipede in your bathroom."

She gasped, put a hand to her mouth. "You killed it, didn't you?"

"You'll never see that particular centipede again."

She sighed with relief. "I couldn't have slept a wink, knowing it was there."

"And if you couldn't have slept, I'm sure I couldn't have either."

He accepted her effusive appreciation, waited until she was out of sight, and grinned a lopsided grin.

He'd found the poor creature clinging to the tiles, probably paralyzed with fear by Mrs. Sawchuck's screams, gathered it into a Kleenex, and released it outdoors.

"Why a woman who wants to bludgeon every living thing chooses to vacation at a country inn is beyond me," he said.

Margaret pulled the menu plan from the shelf. "Out of curiosity, where did you put the centipede this time?"

"Oh, I found him a rotting log. I'm sure he'll find it to his liking."

"That was thoughtful of you, Rudley."

Norman and Geraldine paused on their way to the dining room.

"By this time tomorrow, you'll be on your camping adventure," Norman said.

"Leaving late afternoon," Rudley said. "In time to set up camp before supper."

"I'm sure you'll have a wonderful time," Geraldine said. "Norman and I have spent many memorable nights under the stars."

Rudley cleared his throat. "I can well imagine." He waited until they were out of earshot, then added, "Although I will try very hard not to."

"What was that, Rudley?"

"Oh, nothing, Margaret. Just muttering to myself."

She folded the menu, tucked it away. "It was nice to see Mr. Carty stop for cocktails. I was afraid he might have trouble fitting in. I don't think we've ever had someone so young. And he seems so bashful."

"He's a respectful young man."

"I hope he hasn't come here to do himself in. I mean, at his age, and all by himself."

Rudley crossed his eyes. "Let's not put a hex on the season. I think he's just a mature, independent sort."

Margaret paused as the Lawrences crossed the lobby. "They seem to be a successful young couple."

"Stylish."

"Quite a change from our usual clientele."

"Once you get past the baggy shorts and dentures, I'm sure they're much the same."

"They seem consumed with appearances."

He tilted his head, smiled. "I imagine if we were to put in some hot tubs, a tanning station, some computer outlets in the dining room, we could attract more of their type. We could have the staff in spandex."

Margaret had taken an aster from the vase and was in the process of trimming the stem. She hit him over the head with it. "Bite your tongue, Rudley."

"You're right, Margaret. The idea of Gregoire in spandex is appalling."

"I think the Lawrences like the inn just as it is. He's an avid fisherman. She seems keen on the local art community."

"Quite right, although I don't think I'd want an inn full of them." He paused as Jack Arnold sauntered in. "Or him."

Margaret shuddered. "Yes, I've noticed him leering at Tiffany and Trudy, and especially at Mrs. Lawrence."

Rudley sniffed. "The man's a skirt-chaser. After a few drinks, Aunt Pearl wouldn't be safe."

She gave the aster an encouraging fluff. "I don't understand how a man turns out that way."

"Poor upbringing," Rudley said. "I, for one, was raised by a father who never entertained a lascivious thought. Except occasionally for my mother, I suppose." He thought about his father, a straightforward, hard-working, old-time family doctor who saw patients day and night. Wouldn't have had time for a lascivious thought if he'd wanted one.

Went to church on Sundays. Demanded that his children be active and productive. Treated his wife with affection and respect. He had no patience with philanderers.

"He mentioned he's divorced."

"He would have to be. I can't imagine any woman in her right mind putting up with his shenanigans."

"At least he's not sneaky about it. I suppose he's a tragic figure."

"I think he's just a twit who got hooked on swilling booze and bothering girls in high school and never grew out of making a nuisance of himself."

"That's tragic, Rudley."

"I suppose."

She touched his arm. "We should be ashamed of ourselves for gossiping about the guests."

Rudley nodded. "Yes, Margaret, they deserve their privacy. As long as they pay their bills and don't undress in the lobby."

Miss Miller and Mr. Simpson called out a hello as they entered the lobby.

"Did you have a nice trip to the islands?"

"Wonderful."

"It was quite an adventure, Mrs. Rudley," said Simpson.

"How was the new boat?" Rudley asked.

Miss Miller smiled. "Your craft showed wonderful stability and responsiveness."

"Able to recover from a ninety-degree list, I gather."

"Heart-stopping," Simpson murmured.

"Perfect," said Miss Miller.

Miss Miller and Mr. Simpson went on into the dining room.

"I am so glad they chose to have their wedding here," Margaret said. She gave Rudley a peck on the cheek. "Isn't it romantic, having a wedding here?"

"Yes, Margaret."

"I can't wait to find out which setting they choose."

"If Miss Miller keeps doing wheelies around the shoal markers, the wedding's going to be in the local emergency room."

"Bite your tongue, Rudley." Margaret left to check on the dining room.

Rudley shook his head. Miss Miller was a spirited young woman — much like Margaret when he first met her. He could still see her sailing over the hedgerows on that chestnut hunter while he stood, hands over his eyes, occasionally taking an anguished peek through his fingers. Margaret was much more sedate these days. Not because she'd lost her spirit, but because she'd come to the conclusion it was unkind to make a horse jump for his oats. She had never supported the fox hunt and had regularly attended meetings and protests with the anti-fox-hunting group at home. That was one of the things that attracted him to Margaret — her kindness.

He had met Margaret in London, England, while studying hotel management. It was love at first sight. He smiled, did a brisk foxtrot behind the desk, snapped himself back and hastily drew out the register as a group of dinner guests passed through the lobby. Margaret loved his nimble feet. Best dancer west of London. Not bad for a boy from Galt. That was the only reason his father hadn't disowned him when he decided to become an innkeeper. He was relieved he hadn't chosen a career in dance. Fine man, his father. But a bit of a stick-in-the-mud.

He paused to watch the pace of the wait staff pick up as the dining room filled. Handsome young Tim, Trudy, now a college student, back for the summer, and Mrs. Millotte. "Stiff old fart," he muttered. "Although she may loosen up now that she's taken up the bongos." He drummed out a little beat on the register, smiled, leaned over the desk.

He and Margaret had owned the Pleasant for over a quarter of a century. The fine old inn with its scattered guest cottages and sublime surroundings was his pride and joy. Everything in apple-pie order, thanks to his strange but incomparable handyman, Lloyd Brawly. The man could have been Dr. Frankenstein's right-hand man, he thought, but since he could lathe a spindle with the best of them, he could stay as long as he wanted to — probably forever.

They all acted as if they planned to stay forever. Sometimes the staff reminded him of a nest of fledglings: They surely had somewhere better to go, but the nest was just too comfortable.

Take Tiffany, he thought. Talented young woman with a master's degree in English literature. She'd just had a book of short stories published — by some obscure feminist press. Nevertheless, he considered the publication an achievement. Tiffany had come to him from Toronto for a summer job five years before. Since then, she'd run through half the eligible bachelors in the vicinity. Rather particular. Much as Mrs. Rudley had been. He smiled. Tim McAuley glided past the door of the dining room. The man would have been on stage at the Royal Alex by now if he hadn't found an outlet for his talent in Margaret's summer theatre. He'd done a wonderful Henry Higgins in *Pygmalion*.

Margaret bustled out from the kitchen with a tray. "Gregoire sent you out some supper," she said. "There's no place for you to sit in the dining room." She deposited the tray on the desk and hurried away.

Rudley lifted the first lid. Spicy tomato bisque. Nice little avocado side salad. He lifted the lid of the entrée, inhaled deeply. Grilled salmon steak with dilled butter, asparagus spears, potatoes lyonnaise. And — he opened the box containing the dessert — Gregoire's exquisite pecan pie. One and a half inches of ambrosia, topped with pecans jostling each other for space.

He pulled up his stool, sat down, spreading his serviette over his knees. Wonderful cook, Gregoire. Damned temperamental though. He sampled the salmon, closed his eyes in bliss. At least he'd stopped experimenting with wild mushrooms. He had to admit they were more flavourful than the cultivated ones, even the ones Lloyd grew in his pile of rotting logs, but they had their drawbacks. We'll have to get in a mycologist one day, he decided, to map out the location of the more poisonous varieties.

He sighed. Tried the salad. The past six months had been perfect. Splendid winter with a traditional sleigh-bell Christmas, tobogganing, and ice fishing. Norman had run into the bramble bush. But no serious harm done. He was able to manipulate his fishing gear well enough with one hand and even managed to catch a fish or two, something he seldom accomplished when the lake was open. Maybe he had better luck because the fish couldn't see him in the winter. "I can imagine it would be rather frightening, staring up into those buck teeth," he muttered.

Lovely spring. The lawns covered with tulips and narcissus, crocuses and hyacinth, daffodils and flags. They had put on their usual Easter parade, and, now, with that beautiful period of spring merging into summer, a wedding. Life was good.

He paused, a perfect piece of avocado hovering. The camping adventure. That was a bit of a bump. But Margaret was enthusiastic. Great girl, Margaret. Impossible to deny her a cherished dream: lying on a damp forest floor, being devoured by mosquitoes. He scowled, then coaxed himself into a smile. In spite of the camping trip, he had to admit the life of an innkeeper was damn near perfect.

Chapter 2

Evelyn Hopper looked up as her husband, Carl, paused in the doorway of her office.

"I'm off," he said. He gave her a feeble smile.

"I'll see you later then." She returned to her work.

He hesitated, started to say something, then left.

Evelyn waited until she heard the door downstairs close, then sat back, tossing her pen onto the desk.

She knew Carl was disappointed she hadn't offered to drive him into Middleton for his dental appointment. She shook her head. It was a dental extraction, for heaven's sake, not brain surgery. Of course, this was the man who wore those ugly glasses because contact lenses *tortured* his eyes and got upset if his socks had seams across the toes.

He'd told her he was going to walk the three miles into town. He couldn't take the car, he said, because he might not be able to drive home after the procedure. She had suggested he take a cab home — he could have taken a cab in, for that matter. It wasn't as if they couldn't afford the fare. He could have hired a registered nurse to accompany him, for all she cared. But she wasn't going to be his chauffeur. And she most definitely wasn't going to be his nurse. She had work to do. She was expecting a call from a client that afternoon.

She studied the image on the monitor — a mockup of a living-room design for a client in Toronto. It was a project that required finesse. The client had lots of money and no taste. They had hired her because the man's boss had recommended her. It would take some sweet-talking to get her way — something she was good at if she wanted to be.

She caught sight of Carl from her office window, trudging along, head down, looking like a whipped puppy.

She'd thought he'd be happy after they moved out into the country. He'd been such a sad sack that last year in the city. But, lately, he seemed even more down in the dumps and increasingly ineffectual. She sighed. She now appreciated what her grandmother meant when she'd told her never to marry a man who couldn't fix the plumbing.

She'd never seen it coming. When she met Carl, he was an up-and-coming advertising executive with plans for launching his own firm. He had a hobby — creative writing. She'd never thought much about it, certainly never imagined it would take over his life. He had a few short stories published, then a novel. Then one day, out of the blue, he announced he planned to make writing his career.

He'd changed in other ways that last year in the city, had become more melancholy, less interested in social interaction. At first she thought — when she had time to think about it — that his dissatisfaction was related to his job. Then he started complaining about the city feeling claustrophobic. At first, she thought his discontent had to do with some romantic notion of the writer in a pastoral setting, then she realized he merely wanted to escape.

She clicked the mouse and altered the colour of the drapes in her virtual living room. Not that she had any regret about abandoning city life. Having a permanent home for the horses was worth the inconvenience of living out here. The real-estate agent had extolled the virtues of living in cottage country, but the proximity of the lake had not been a factor in choosing the property — she didn't care much for the water. Nor did she see any advantage in being close to the various inns. Most of them had been in the same hands for years. And those hands were either unaware of the dowdiness of their establishments, or for some reason, felt obliged to maintain them in their original condition. While she received the occasional contract from the villages in the area, the bulk of her work remained in the larger cities.

Carl loved the farm. Of course, she thought, he would have loved a shack, anyplace devoid of stress and responsibility. She clicked on the davenport and moved it across the room, added a credenza.

Their daughter, Terri, she was afraid, had too much of her father in her. She'd given Terri every advantage, but the girl lacked polish and poise. She had chosen a nondescript program in university, a soft degree in the humanities with a few bird courses in the sciences. How she expected to forge a career out of that potpourri, Evelyn couldn't imagine. Terri was twenty-two, and reasonably attractive — although she would have been more attractive if she'd shed that layer of baby fat. Evelyn had encouraged her in sports, but the only thing she'd stuck with was horseback riding. The horses were the slender thread that held them together. Evelyn moved the mouse into the client's hallway. Terri had terrible taste in men. She shook her head. Maybe that was something else they had in common.

Chapter 3

Tim and Gregoire approached the front desk. Tim looked pointedly at his watch. Rudley gave them a long look. "Yes?"

"Time for you to leave for your camping trip," said Tim.

Rudley whipped out a checklist. "Are you prepared to mind the store while we're away?"

"You will never know you have been away," said Gregoire.

"If someone inquires about reservations, you must check the master list. Margaret has a master plan for each room and cottage. You will be able to tell at a glance what is available and when."

"It sounds like a mistress plan," said Tim.

Rudley's eyes crossed. "And dinner reservations."

"I can handle that with my eyes closed," said Tim.

"I trust you've solidified the entertainment plans?"

"Miss Miller and Mr. Simpson have that in hand," said Tim. "Mr. Bole will be performing a puppet show as dinner theatre — *Waiting for Godot*. After dinner, we will proceed to the canasta tournament, and, as the grand finale, Snakes and Ladders."

"That should throw Mrs. Sawchuck into a panic."

"We've prepared a special board for her table," said Tim. "Slides and Ladders."

"Good. The last thing we need is a padded wagon showing up."

Norman Phipps-Walker came down the stairs with a bag slung over his shoulder.

"Ready for the grand excursion, Norman?" Rudley asked.

"Ready. I have my fishing equipment. Also a camera and a recording device. I understand there's a good population of owls up at Briar Point." He paused. "Brilliant of that young lady to start her charter."

Rudley nodded. "I don't know if I'd call Doretta a young lady. She's in her forties and built like a brick outhouse."

"Someone told me she used to be a grade-school teacher," Norman said. "She must have a gentle heart."

Rudley nodded. "I understand the children loved her once they got over the fact she could lift a piano with one hand."

Bonnie and Tee Lawrence entered the lobby at that moment, she in a tailored pantsuit with coordinated scarf, he in khakis, a plaid shirt, and a vest with many pockets. He carried a Bob Izumi fishing rod and reel.

Margaret bustled out from the kitchen with two picnic baskets. "Norman, Mr. Lawrence, here's your supper."

Norman took his basket. "Are you going on Doretta's fishing charter?" he asked Tee.

Tee hesitated. "Yes."

"Well," said Norman. "No need for both of us to drive. You can come with me."

"No need for either of you to drive," said Margaret. "Lloyd's going into town for the Monster Marathon at the Regent. He'll drive you in and pick you up later."

Bonnie looked distressed. "But I wanted to drive Tee in."

Tee rolled his eyes. "I've told you, Bonnie, there's no need for you to drive me."

"But I was planning to stop by the pharmacy and pick up the latest brides' magazines," Bonnie fretted. "I was hoping to spend the evening getting some ideas for Miss Miller's wedding."

"You don't have to do that tonight," said Tee.

Margaret brightened. "As it happens, I have some recent copies. We're putting on *Father of the Bride* this season. I'll be happy to get them for you."

Tee patted Bonnie on the shoulder as she continued to fuss. "There, you can plan to your heart's content."

"But…"

Tee kissed her on the cheek. "And since you don't have to drive me into town or pick me up later, you'll have even more time to plan the wedding."

Bonnie looked crestfallen.

"I'll get those magazines right away," said Margaret. "And I'll ask Lloyd to drop you off. He's just finishing his dinner. He should be ready in a few minutes."

"There you are," said Tee. He gave Bonnie another peck, smiled. "Have a nice dinner, and I'll see you later." He headed for the door.

"You could have dinner with Geraldine," said Norman. "I'm sure she'd love to have you join her. She can tell you about our wedding. Avian motif. Bird songs in the background, that sort of thing. Afterwards, we provided a bird buffet so our feathered friends could also enjoy the occasion. Perhaps you'd like to include something like that in Miss Miller's wedding."

Bonnie looked as if she were going to cry.

"Just give her a buzz," Norman said as he turned to catch up with Tee. "She likes to dine at seven."

Lloyd came out of the dining room.

"You know you're going to drop Mr. Lawrence and Norman at the dock," Rudley said.

"Yes'm."

"What movies are you going to see?"

"*Godzilla* and *The Monster who Devoured Cleveland*."

"Sounds horrific."

Bonnie was still standing in front of the desk, clutching her handbag to her chest.

"Don't worry," said Rudley. "He's a fine driver and not dangerous in any way we know of."

Margaret arrived at the desk carrying a pile of magazines. "I found you six copies." She plopped the bundle into Bonnie's arms.

"Thank you, Mrs. Rudley," Bonnie said in a small voice. "I think I'll go now and freshen up for dinner."

"Mrs. Lawrence seems upset," said Margaret as she watched her walk down the front steps, shoulders hunched. "But I'm sure the magazines I found will do. None of them is more than a year old."

"She's a rather delicate little thing," Rudley said.

"He doesn't seem particularly sensitive to her."

"Opposites do attract, Margaret. Look at Miss Miller and Mr. Simpson."

"Yes, Rudley, but Miss Miller and Mr. Simpson clearly respect each other. Mr. Lawrence seems almost condescending."

"Some men are beasts."

"Perhaps being here, with our example, meeting other exemplary couples, perhaps that will rub off on Mr. Lawrence."

"Or perhaps on both of them. He can stop being so condescending, and she can stop being such a ninnyhammer."

Tim cleared his throat. "Your camping trip?"

"Your gear is waiting for you on the back porch," said Gregoire.

Margaret pried the pen from Rudley's hand. "Time to go, Rudley." She beamed. "I'm so looking forward to this experience."

Jack Arnold shoved his wallet into his pocket. He had his hand on the doorknob, then hesitated and turned back. He grabbed a bottle of Glenlivet, slopped two fingers into a tumbler, saluted the bottle, and downed the drink in one go. One for the road.

He glanced at his watch. Eight-thirty. He was headed into town, hoping to catch some action at the hotel. The fact that he'd killed half the bottle that day didn't worry him. He'd been drinking and driving for years. If the cops in Sarnia couldn't detect he was DUI, the hicks out here wouldn't. He'd just finished a big dinner and felt quite capable of steering several tons of metal along a winding country road.

He put his glass down on the table by the door and left.

Great evening, he thought. Warm. Half-moon. Water lapping against the dock. Not a soul in sight. He heard muted laughter as he passed the inn. They were having some kind of games night. He'd heard someone mention Snakes and Ladders. He hadn't played that game since grade school and couldn't imagine why the whole inn would crowd into the drawing room for that sort of entertainment. Of course, most of the guests were either infirm like the Sawchucks, or old nuts like the Phipps-Walkers, or just plain weird like that red-headed woman with the thick glasses. Educated woman. Saucy. He didn't like saucy, educated women. The laughter faded as he approached the parking lot. Here it was just the frogs and crickets. He belched and climbed into his vintage Cadillac.

The Caddy was old and a bit beat up, with dents and scratches here and there he'd never bothered fixing. He liked to think of the car as an extension of himself — getting along in years with the bumps and bruises from a life lived hard and a little recklessly but still with a charge in the engine.

He pulled out of the driveway, paused to decide which road to take. The one to the left ran along the shore before curving to meet the main road. The one to the right led up through the woods, he believed, before meeting the highway a mile or so along. He glanced to his right, caught sight of a familiar figure hurrying up the road in the distance. Hell of a time to go for a walk, he thought. He turned the wheel to the left and set out along the shore road.

Trevor Rudley reached down the back of his pajamas, pulled out an insect, held it out. "What do you think this is, Margaret?"

She squinted in the dim light. "I think it's a pillbug."

"How am I supposed to sleep with all of these insects crawling over me?"

She took the bug from him, released it into a corner of the tent. "They're just innocent denizens of the soil. We have a net to keep the mosquitoes off."

He started to crawl out of his sleeping bag. "Let's go home."

"We just got here." She gave him a reproachful look. "This isn't about the insects. You like insects. You just don't like being away from the front desk." She snuggled up to him. "Rudley, it's wonderful here.

The clean, earthy fragrance of the forest carpet, the crickets chirping, the owls hooting, the brook gurgling over its rock bed."

"We could get that from the back porch."

"Privacy. We can't get that from the back porch."

He thought about that for a moment, smiled. "I have to admit you're right about that, Margaret. No Lloyd sneaking up on me, depriving me of two years of life, no Gregoire nagging me over cilantro and fennel root. No Aunt Pearl suffocating me with her whisky fumes."

She sighed. "Alone at last."

He plucked a slug from his arm. "Virtually."

A twig snapped.

Rudley froze, slug poised.

"It is us."

Rudley sighed. "Come."

The tent flap opened. Tim poked his head in. Gregoire hovered at his shoulder.

"We're not here," Rudley said. "We're camping in Algonquin Park."

Tim ignored him. "Shall I take away the supper dishes?"

"Please."

"Did you enjoy the trout?" Gregoire asked.

"Excellent."

"I grilled it over an open fire. Just as if you'd caught it and cooked it yourself."

Gregoire ducked outside the tent, came back with a picnic basket. "We brought you a thermos of coffee, raspberry scones, and a cognac nightcap."

"Wonderful."

"And what would you like for breakfast?"

"Surprise us."

"Should we expect you home by noon?"

Rudley gave Margaret a jaunty smile. "Unless we decide to toss our unmentionables into the bramble bush and cavort in the brook, or braid daisy chains."

"I really don't want to hear this," said Gregoire.

"And how are things back at the ranch?"

"You will be pleased to know everything is functioning as usual," said Tim.

"That's enough to make me shudder," said Rudley. He gave them an expectant look as they lingered. "You may leave now."

"Thank you for the treats," said Margaret. She turned to Rudley. "Wasn't that sweet of them?"

"They're like children," said Rudley. "You can't get away from them."

"Nor would we want to."

Rudley crossed his eyes. "Why do I sometimes feel like the headmaster of a school for incorrigibles? I'm surprised Tiffany hasn't shown up."

"Tiffany said she was making fudge this evening."

They finished their snack. Rudley collapsed back against his pillow. "Being an innkeeper can be a trial at times."

Margaret poured two glasses of cognac. "Oh, you love it." She handed him a glass. "Bottoms up."

Carl Hopper woke to the sound of an approaching car engine. Or was it the sound of silence following the sound of an engine? Light pierced the gap between the curtains. The light cut a swath across the window, then was extinguished.

The room was dark. He fumbled for the light switch, knocked a glass over, gave up. He was sitting in the recliner in his living room. His jaw throbbed.

He sorted through a grainy set of mental images. He'd gone to Middleton for a dental appointment. The dentist had given him a prescription for Tylenol #3. He'd gone to the library, taken a couple of the pills, sat in a dark corner, and rested for an hour. After that, he'd made his way to the hotel for a bowl of soup. Then he started to walk home. A guest at the West Wind had come upon him weaving along the road and had given him a ride to the laneway. He'd fallen asleep on the couch, woken sometime later in pain. He'd taken two more pills and sat down in the recliner, meaning to watch the evening news. That was the last thing he remembered before the engine woke him.

He ratcheted the recliner into a sitting position as he heard footsteps on the veranda. The door burst open. He caught a glimpse of Evelyn as she switched on the light in the hallway and hammered up the stairs. He reached for the table lamp, finally located it, and turned it on. The glass he had tipped over had, fortunately, been empty. He looked around for his pain pills, spotted them on the floor a few feet from his chair. He was trying to figure out if he had the wherewithal to get up and get them when Evelyn came downstairs.

"Evelyn?"

She turned, startled.

He grinned. "I dropped my pills. Could you get them for me? And a glass of water, please?"

Her surprise turned to anger. "Get your own pills, you pathetic..." The words dissolved in an explosion of disgust. She spun and slammed out the door.

He shrank back against the cushions, stunned. Finally, he got up, made his way to the kitchen, ran the tap for a glass of water, and dropped into a chair at the table. Gave a mirthless laugh as he realized he had left his pills in the living room. He wobbled back to the living room, bent to pick up the bottle. The change in position brought on a wave of vertigo. "OK, soldier," he muttered, "you can do this." He snared the bottle, then grabbed the edge of the coffee table and levered himself up. He went back to the kitchen and took the pills. He sat down, resting his head against the wall. The wing of his glasses bit into his temple. He took them off and stuffed them into his breast pocket.

He dozed off, woke to a high-pitched whinny. He sat for a few minutes, trying to clear his head.

He thought of the expression on Evelyn's face. Anger? Surprise? He swallowed hard. Maybe pure hatred. He shook his head. Evelyn didn't hate him. Maybe impatience. She'd been impatient with him lately. He paused. Maybe for a long time.

He needed to talk to her. He reviewed what he would say. Talking to Evelyn was like walking on eggshells these days.

He got up and went out onto the veranda. Evelyn's car was in its usual spot. He surmised she was in the stable. Probably telling the horses her secrets. He shrugged. Lately, he'd taken to confiding in the horses himself. He sagged against the pillar, deflated. God, he needed a cigarette. He patted himself down, searching for his Player's Regulars, found them in his hip pocket. There were four cigarettes left, all bent, two broken at the filter. He removed one of the salvageable ones, straightened it, and lit up. He inhaled deeply. The cigarette comforted him, gave him a modicum of clarity. He dragged on it as he made his way down the path to the barn.

The stable door was open.

"Evelyn?"

No response.

He plunged the cigarette into a pot of sand by the door and entered the stable. He felt his way along the box stalls past Gert and Maisie. Bob plucked at his shirt as he passed.

"Sorry," he mumbled, "I didn't bring you anything."

Ned's stall was empty. He stood there, staring into the empty space as if he expected the horse to be hiding in a corner, then backed away. He supposed Evelyn had taken Ned for one of her nocturnal jaunts up the laneway. She did that when she was trying to sort something out. The horses were her soulmates. Sometimes, he thought she loved the horses more than she loved him. He laughed, a laugh that ended in a sob. He knew she loved the horses more than she loved him.

He started back toward the door, blinded by tears, tripped and fell violently to the floor. He lay there against the cement, feeling lonely and abused.

Finally, he picked himself up and limped back to the house. He went to the liquor cabinet, poured an ounce of Scotch and downed it in one gulp. He poured another and took it to the couch. He turned on the television, hoping there might be something on that would cheer him up, found himself staring at a blurry version of something called *Lady Hoggers*. He turned the television off, took a slug of his drink. The Scotch tasted good. He comforted himself with the knowledge that his daughter, Terri, was coming home the next day. He hoped to God Evelyn would be in a better mood by then. He hated Terri to know things weren't a bed of roses at home. He finished the drink and lay down, waiting for her to return.

Tiffany sat on a stool, stirring a pot of fudge. The aroma of chocolate filled the kitchen. "This is like being at a slumber party."

Gregoire checked the oven, then poured coffee all around. "I will have to take your word for that."

Tiffany gave the fudge a few lazy swirls, then rested the spoon along the handle of the pot. "When I was a teenager, my friend Hortense and I would make fudge every Friday night while my parents were out shopping."

Tim hoisted his coffee. "So this is like having the parents out shopping."

"The parents were most anxious about how we are managing here," said Gregoire.

Tim took out his notebook. "Very well, I would say. We've taken nine dinner reservations, checked in two guests, confirmed six reservations, and solved the plumbing problem in the Elm Pavilion. Thanks to yours truly."

"I never thought you had it in you to be a plumber," said Gregoire.

"Having three old ladies with a compromised commode is a great motivator." Tim reviewed his notes. "Caught a mouse headed toward the Sawchucks' room. Live release. Tiffany fed the cat. Mr. Simpson walked Albert. I would say everything is in order."

"I hope Mr. and Mrs. Rudley will be all right," said Tiffany.

"They are only three hundred yards from the back porch," said Gregoire.

"That's quite a long way in the woods. They could be attacked by a bear."

The fudge began to boil. Tim reached for the spoon.

"Perhaps we should check on them during the night," said Tiffany. "We could take turns."

Gregoire turned to Tiffany. "Believe me, there is nothing to worry about."

Tim opened the refrigerator, scanned the shelves. "I thought we had some roast beef left over."

"I gave you the last for Mr. Carty. You said he wanted a doggy bag."

"He's a bottomless pit," said Tim.

"He's a growing boy. There is chicken and ham if you want a sandwich."

"Let's have chicken sandwiches and talk about the wedding," said Tim. "That will take Tiffany's mind off the Rudleys being gnawed by bears."

"It is marvellous," said Gregoire, "Miss Miller and Mr. Simpson choosing to have their wedding here."

"It's so romantic," said Tiffany.

"Knowing Miss Miller, it should be an eventful affair," said Tim. He paused. "I hope no one gets murdered."

There was a long silence.

"That's a horrible thought," said Tiffany.

"But not outlandish," said Tim.

"Nothing like that will possibly happen," said Gregoire.

They turned to the rat-a-tat-tat of steps across the dining room floor.

"Aunt Pearl," said Tim.

She went immediately to the stove, peered into the pot. "Fudge. Wonderful. I just bombed out in the Snakes and Ladders tournament. A big one. Anaconda, I think." She nudged Gregoire "You wouldn't have a little drink for an old lady?"

"How about a nice glass of cranberry juice?"

"How about a Black Russian?" She smiled as he dug into the cupboard. "How's my darling niece getting along?"

"She's enjoying herself immensely," said Tim.

Tiffany took the fudge off the burner, set it aside to cool. "We were talking about the wedding."

"I'm looking forward to that." Pearl took the glass Gregoire held out.

"We were just saying something always seems to happen when Miss Miller is around," said Gregoire.

Pearl waved that off. "Don't blame Miss Miller. Blame Rudley. We haven't had a week without sirens blaring since he bought the place." She paused. "I can still see that unfortunate man dangling from the ski lift."

Tiffany mixed a teaspoon of vanilla into the fudge, poured it into a pan, and set it aside. "I'm glad I wasn't here to see that."

Pearl tested her drink, gave it a nod of approval. "The wedding's going to be a real wingding. I'll never forget my wedding."

They leaned toward her expectantly.

"St. Albans. Great old thing from the seventeenth century. I wore a full-length gown with seed pearls. The bridesmaids were a veritable rainbow of pastels. Winnie and his attendants in morning suits. Cute little flower girl — fifth cousin or something. Cute little ring bearer. John Elgie from Coventry, the best church organist outside of London, played the wedding march. Lovely reception at my parents' country home. Then off to a honeymoon on the continent."

"Sounds lovely," said Tiffany,

Aunt Pearl thought for a moment. "Actually, it was a real bore. How Mother roped me into that, I can't imagine. By the time it was over, Winnie and I were wishing we'd eloped." She drained her glass. "So a night in the woods. That's Margaret's camping trip."

"I think it's just a trial run," said Tim.

Gregoire sniffed. "Yes, it is a trial run. Mr. Rudley is hoping Margaret will be so put off by the experience, she will beg him not to repeat it."

Tiffany smiled. "I think they really just wanted some time to themselves."

"I have to admit, Margaret, it is rather relaxing here."

Margaret emitted a soft snore.

"So much for lying awake deep into the night, listening to owls and so forth." Rudley folded his arms behind his head, stared up at the nylon ceiling. Time was, a tent was canvas, he thought. Wonderful chemical smell.

He'd loved camping out when he was a boy. He and his pal Squiggy Ross would hike up into the woods, pitch a tent, do a little fishing. They'd fry the fish over an open fire, bake potatoes in the coals. Toast a few marshmallows. Take turns telling ghost stories. No one thought anything of letting two young boys go off into the woods overnight. It was a more innocent time.

He smiled. His old friend Squiggy, the blue-eyed boy with the blond curls and gap-toothed smile. Squiggy was still camping out, but now it was in downtown Galt, minus teeth, minus hair, with a cap between his knees, collecting change for a cheap bottle of wine.

Like most boys, Squiggy wanted to be a fireman. Rudley had always assumed he'd be a doctor like his father. Then he took a summer job at the Baltimore Hotel and he knew he'd found his calling.

The Baltimore was a magical place. He relished entering the lobby every morning. The gleaming oak hardwood floor with its scarlet runner. The long solid oak front desk with its leather-bound register, and the bell you struck smartly for service. The amber wainscoting and old-fashioned wallpaper with its pastoral motif. The umbrella stand just inside the front door. He chuckled. Back then, it was safe to leave a good umbrella in a public stand. Everybody in town knew your umbrella. They'd beat anyone to a pulp if they caught it on them. The dining room, one step down through frosted French doors. The aroma of bacon and eggs and toast. The wide staircase with its curved banister. The elegant old elevator with its brass gate. He'd started as a scullery boy that first summer, worked his way up to janitor. The year before he left to go to college he'd graduated to bellhop and thought he knew everything there was to know about the operation of a hotel.

His father had not been delighted when he informed him he'd be forgoing medical school. "Innkeeper," he'd said. "Probably better than being a vaudevillian — although not much." He'd worked in grander hotels during his apprenticeship, interned at more pretentious resorts, but not until he laid eyes on the Pleasant did he feel the thrill of having rediscovered the Baltimore.

He considered his father's words. Of course, he could have been a vaudevillian. He was almost as good a dancer as Fred Astaire. At least as good as Gene Kelly. Kelly didn't have the body for dance, in his opinion. Always looked like a bull pirouetting about. He shrugged. Great dancers were a dime a dozen. "How many great innkeepers do you know?" he asked Margaret. She did not respond. He smiled. He knew what she would say: "You're the best, Rudley." That's what she would say.

The fudge was ready. Tim helped himself to a piece. "I saw Officer Owens in town today." He winked at Gregoire. "He looked rather dashing."

Tiffany gave Tim a frosty look. "How very nice for you."

Gregoire gave the counter a wipe. "It is better than having him here, which we do all too frequently." He paused. "He is always welcome, of course, in his unofficial capacity."

Tiffany looked away. "Officer Owens' activities are of no concern to me."

Tim and Gregoire exchanged glances.

After a long pause, Tiffany said, "I've had second thoughts about Officer Owens. I'm not sure we're compatible."

Gregoire rolled his eyes. "Just last week you were telling us it was refreshing to have an uncomplicated relationship. You said that was the problem with your previous situations. That your beaux were oozing with existential angst and performance anxieties about their iambic pentameters and arpeggios."

She gave him a defiant look, then relented. "You're right. I did say that."

Tim made a pretence of searching his memory. "Let me see, you said you liked the fact he was transparent, that you didn't feel he was playing games. You said he was easy to be with. Thoughtful. Unlike Officer Semple who, although he could play a musical instrument, was self-involved."

She folded her arms. "True."

Tim raised his brows. "So?"

"He's not sufficiently challenging."

Gregoire removed his apron. "I do not understand this business of a challenge." He balled up his cap, stuffed it into his pocket. "You are attracted to someone. You do things together you enjoy. You go to fine restaurants. You eat magnificent food, drink excellent wines. Perhaps you prepare gourmet meals together. You go to the theatre. After, you stop at the café for dessert and cappuccino. You travel, sample the local cuisine. What is it with these complications and challenges?"

Tiffany looked at him, bewildered.

Tim straightened his tie. "What Gregoire is trying to say is that you don't need to subject your soul to constant nitpicking. You hook up with someone you like and go with the flow.".

Gregoire sniffed. "I think I said it more eloquently."

Tiffany turned away, turned back, lower lip quivering. "The truth is I've learned something disturbing about Officer Owens. Something unforgivable."

Gregoire's eyes blazed. "He has been unfaithful. I will give him a piece of my mind."

Tiffany shook her head.

Tim cleared his throat. "He drinks too much."

"No. He's a veritable teetotaler."

"He has struck you." Gregoire balled the corners of his jacket into his fists. "I will tear him from limb to limb."

"No. Officer Owens is a gentleman."

Tim took a turn around the kitchen, stopped in front of Tiffany. "Let's see. He doesn't use deodorant. He turns into a werewolf when the moon is full."

She closed her eyes. "He hunts."

Tim and Gregoire looked at one another.

"He's the most perfect man I've ever met and he kills animals." She began to wail.

An owl hooted. Twigs snapped. Margaret sat bolt upright. "Rudley, what was that?"

He responded without opening his eyes. "In my dreams, it was a Siberian yak."

She grabbed him by the shoulder. "No, really, there's something thrashing about in the bushes."

Rudley crawled out of his sleeping bag, groped for the flashlight, fumbled to the tent flap on hands and knees. He thrust the flashlight through the slit, caught the tail end of a fleeing creature. He snapped the flashlight off.

"What was it, Rudley?"

"I think it was a deer."

"It sounded too big to be a deer. Are you sure it wasn't a bear?"

"I don't think so, Margaret." He backed into his sleeping bag. "Even if it was, it was running away from us."

She sighed. "That's a sensible way to look at it."

"I'm always sensible."

She let that go. "Good night, Rudley."

"Good night, Margaret."

Chapter 4

Gregoire woke at four, a few minutes before his alarm was set to go off, and headed for the shower. The early hours required by his job had never been a problem for him. His mother said he hadn't slept more than four or five hours a night since he was born. He enjoyed a half-hour nap in the afternoon and always woke refreshed.

Tim's door was ajar. He paused, listened, chuckled. The elegant Tim snored.

He climbed into the shower, turned the water to tepid.

He considered Tiffany's problem as he worked his hair into a lather. Officer Owens was a nice man, patient, respectful. But he shoots Bambi, he thought, and Booboo. He paused, clutching the bar of soap to his chest. The man was a philistine.

He reviewed the menu for the day: prime rib, rack of lamb... Frowned. "You are as much of a murderer as he is," he muttered.

He turned off the shower and tumbled out, reaching for his towel. His dark curls sprang out like corkscrews. He stared at his reflection in the mirror, tried to smooth the disobedient curls with one hand. He pulled on his bathrobe, returned to his room, parted the curtains to check the weather.

Dawn threw a sheet of silver over the lake. Rocks and trees lurked in the gloom along the shallows.

He treasured this time of morning. Before the fishermen invaded his kitchen for their thermoses of coffee. Before Tim flitted through the dining room, bringing the full glare of the sun — Tim brought the sun even on cloudy days. Before the clatter of dishes broke the silence. Before the ovens diluted the subtlety of the natural fragrances. Before everyone started blundering around. He liked people, but this fragment of the day belonged to him. He put on his whites, captured his hair under his cap, and tiptoed into the hallway. He paused at Tim's door. "You snore," he whispered.

Lloyd rolled out of his cot in the tool shed behind the inn. He had a room in the bunkhouse but he liked to sleep in the open, and the tool shed was almost as good as being outdoors. Mrs. Rudley didn't mind him living in the tool shed but insisted that he move into the bunkhouse once it got cold. Mrs. Rudley worried about him. She worried about everybody, but he knew she worried about him especially because she thought he was an orphan. He wasn't, but, since he had told her he was, he couldn't take it back. At first, he thought he couldn't tell her the truth because she might decide he didn't need all those extra pieces of pie if he had parents. But now he realized he couldn't tell her because knowing he had lied to her would hurt her feelings. He knew she would find out someday, probably when his parents died. Someone would put a notice in the paper and Mrs. Rudley read the local paper every morning. He decided that the only way to shield Mrs. Rudley from the truth would be to have her die before his parents did. But he didn't want that to happen either. He liked Mrs. Rudley. He comforted himself with the knowledge that the day of reckoning lay in the distant future: Mrs. Rudley's mother had lived a long time and his grandmother was still living. He calculated it might be fifty years before his parents passed on, and, by that time, Mrs. Rudley's memory might not be very good. Besides, he would be old by then too and Mrs. Rudley always said it was important to be kind to old people.

 He watched a grey squirrel work its way down the pine tree, then picked up his towel and went outside to his camp shower. He would rather have washed in the lake as he had for years, but last year Mrs. Rudley told him he couldn't. She said the soap wasn't good for the fish. He guessed it wasn't, but, since he was the only one who bathed in the lake, he didn't think it would do any harm. He thought the real reason Mrs. Rudley had barred him from the lake was that a lady with a cottage on the point had complained that she saw a naked man in the lake while she was watching the deer with her binoculars. He could have showered in the bunkhouse but he liked to be outdoors.

He showered, dressed, and hung his towel on a tree limb to dry. He was hungry but he wanted pancakes and Gregoire wouldn't have the griddle ready until nearly seven. He got out the cultivator, planning to work on the flower beds at the front of the inn. Then he would go in for a coffee and a bun until Gregoire could fix his pancakes. He rounded the corner of the inn, stopped.

A man lay on his back on the wicker lounge on the veranda, his hat tipped over his eyes. Lloyd leaned the cultivator against the wall and climbed the steps to the veranda.

"Yoo hoo."

The man mumbled, waved him away.

Lloyd shook the man by the shoulder. "Yoo hoo."

Jack Arnold pushed his hat back. He was unshaven and stank of stale booze. "What in hell do you want?"

"People'll be coming in soon for breakfast."

Arnold stared at him. "What time is it?"

"Late. Almost six-thirty."

Arnold pulled his hat back down to shield his eyes against the sunlight. "Christ, what are you doing up at this hour?"

"Things to do. You stay here all night?"

Arnold sighed. "I guess so."

Lloyd grinned. "I like sleeping outside too, but Mrs. Rudley doesn't like it. She says I'll get pneumonia."

Arnold turned his head, groaned, massaged his neck. "I don't know about sleeping outdoors but I wouldn't recommend sleeping on this thing." He gestured toward the door. "I don't suppose I could get a cup of coffee."

Lloyd pointed to the trail of mud up the steps and across the veranda. "You got mud on your shoes."

Arnold cocked his head to look down. "Guess I do." He yawned. "Maybe I'll just wait until the dining room opens."

"I can get you some coffee, but you can't go into the dining room with your boots all muddy."

Arnold looked at the veranda. "I guess I did track it all over."

"And on the cushions," said Lloyd, pointing to the lounge.

Arnold managed to look sheepish. "Forget the coffee. I'll go down to my cabin and call for room service when the dining room opens."

"If you go down, I'll bring you some coffee, but you'll have to leave your shoes outside until you can clean them."

Arnold laughed. "You have a housekeeper, don't you?" He scrubbed a hand across his lips. "God, my mouth tastes like a garbage can. They must have snuck me something cheap."

"I'll get you the coffee and clean your shoes. Tiffany's got a lot of cleaning."

Arnold lay back. "Sounds good, buddy. I'll catch a nap until you get back."

Lloyd went around to the back porch and into the kitchen where he told his story to Gregoire.

"The man is a pig," Gregoire fumed. He poured coffee into an insulated mug. "This is good enough for him. I will not have him smashing the good china over the veranda." He pinched his nostrils. "I can smell his foul body from here."

Lloyd took the coffee to the veranda. Arnold had fallen asleep. He put the coffee down, tugged off Arnold's shoes. He took them around to the side of the house, hosed them down, and set them aside. He pulled the soiled cushion out from under Arnold's feet, took it to the back porch where he laid it on the railing to dry. He brought the hose around to the veranda and began to wash down the steps.

Tim wheeled around the corner from the bunkhouse. He stopped and stared at Arnold, who had flopped onto his side and was drooling on his shirt. "What's he doing here?"

"Don't know," said Lloyd. "Was here when I got here."

"He looks as if he spent the night in a pigsty. He's got mud all over his pant legs. Where'd he get that from?"

"Don't know," Lloyd said, "but he got mud all over the veranda."

"I hope he doesn't plan to go into the dining room. I'll boot him into the next lake if he does."

"Told him he couldn't."

Tim gave Arnold a disparaging look and went on into the kitchen. Gregoire was cracking eggs into a mixing bowl.

"Is it ready?"

Gregoire gave him an impatient wave. "I have the popovers coming out of the oven in precisely thirty seconds. I will be serving them with strawberries and fresh Devon cream. Then pigs in the blankets with citrus chutney. They will think they are in their honeymoon cottage in Cornwall."

"Tea, then, instead of coffee?"

Gregoire made a face. "I am afraid the fantasy ends there. If Mr. Rudley misses his coffee, it will be a horror show in here."

Tim helped himself to the strawberries. "I hope they had a good night."

Gregoire opened the oven and pulled out the popovers. "They are probably aching in every joint and covered with insect bites and poison ivy." He took out a carafe, filled it with coffee. "Now, if you will stop eating the strawberries, perhaps you could take this to them."

Margaret opened her eyes, smiled. "Rudley, isn't that cute?"

"Yes, Margaret," he murmured, "cute."

"No, look." She shook him by the shoulder, pointed to the silhouette of a chipmunk posed against the tent. "Look at him. He must know we have some crumbs."

Rudley raised himself on one elbow. "I don't think you should feed him. There's plenty for him to eat. We don't want him to become dependent."

"I don't think a few crumbs will destroy his initiative." She opened the tent flap, scattered the crumbs from their midnight snack. "It's going to be a lovely day. What a wonderful idea to camp out."

"It was." He slithered out of his sleeping bag. "But now I have to go to the bathroom." He put on his shoes and crawled out of the tent on hands and knees.

"Mind the tree roots."

"Yes, Margaret." He stretched, took a lungful of air, paused to indulge a frog that had stopped in his path. "Get along now," he whispered. "There's some urgency in my situation."

The frog blinked, gathered itself, and sailed off into the Mayapple.

Rudley completed his business, paused to look down toward the inn. The lake revealed itself in dancing patterns of blue through the leaves. Phipps-Walker would be out in his rowboat. Soon the dining room would come alive. And soon, Tim would be up with a breakfast tray. Breakfast in the tent, then he'd be glad to get back to the inn. Taking leave of his responsibilities for one night was quite all right but sufficient.

A woodpecker drummed on a tree ahead of him. He meandered along, looking up into the trees, caught sight of the bird crisscrossing halfway up the trunk. He grinned, whistled a few bars of "Oh, What a Beautiful Mornin'." He'd forgotten how lovely the woods were. He'd been telling guests that for years, but it had been some time since he'd enjoyed a stroll up here. He ambled along, paused here and there to examine the texture of the bark, identify an insect, watch the voles scurry along under the leaf blanket.

A grosbeak warbled a greeting. He turned, scanning the trees for the bird, stumbled over a stump, and pitched headlong into the undergrowth.

"Damn." He scrambled up, brushing off his clothes. Paused, jaw dropping. "What the hell?"

Carl Hopper woke to sunlight streaming through the window. He shut his eyes, grabbed his head in both hands. He rolled to his side and promptly fell to the floor. He opened his eyes, saw a blurry version of a Persian rug and the underside of a coffee table. He decided he was lying on the floor beside the living room couch.

He struggled to his feet using the coffee table and couch for support. He patted his breast pocket for his glasses, felt around under the couch cushions, finally gave up, and headed toward the kitchen, grabbing the back of the recliner as a wave of vertigo pitched him to his right. He waited until he felt steadier, then forged ahead. He reached the kitchen, pulled down a mug from the rack, juggled it as it tried to slip through his fingers.

He turned on the coffee pot. It rewarded him with a sterile hiss. He pulled out the basket, checked the reservoir. He was standing there, frowning at the basket of spent grounds when a brisk knock at the kitchen door brought Roslyn, the housekeeper.

"Morning, Mr. Hopper. I brought your paper." She put the newspaper down on the kitchen table.

"No coffee," he said by way of greeting.

"I guess Mrs. Hopper forgot to get it ready last night." Roslyn put her bag down, took the basket from his hands, rinsed it, rinsed the pot, and took down the coffee canister.

Carl sank into a chair at the table while Roslyn prepared the coffee. She turned the pot on, then went to the refrigerator and poured him a glass of orange juice. She set it on the table in front of him.

"If you don't mind me saying so, Mr. Hopper, you don't look so good."

He gave her an apologetic smile. "Bad day yesterday, Roslyn. I had a tooth yanked. I fell asleep on the couch."

She took a long look at him. "You look as if you slept in Drummie's dirt pile."

He squinted at his shirt. "I fell." He took a drink of the orange juice, held it in his dry mouth for a few moments before swallowing. "Those pills the dentist gave me threw me for a loop."

She had her head in the refrigerator. "Do you want your bacon and eggs?"

He felt his jaw. "I don't know. I think my mouth is too sore for anything."

"How about some scrambled eggs?" She got out the fixings without waiting for an answer. "Will Mrs. Hopper be wanting something?"

He drew the newspaper toward him, patting his breast pocket for his glasses. "I don't know."

"Is she upstairs?"

He hesitated. "I don't know."

She gave him a look of affectionate exasperation. "I'll go take a look."

He gave her his best little-boy smile. "Roslyn, could you take a look around for my glasses? They might be on the table by my recliner."

She patted him on the shoulder and took off upstairs. She came down, circled through the living room, and returned to the kitchen.

"Mrs. Hopper's not upstairs," she said, "and I didn't see your glasses."

"She must have gone riding." He stared at the paper, thought about asking Roslyn to get the spare pair from his desk, then decided that would be pushing his luck.

Roslyn poured a cup of coffee, added double cream, and put it on the table in front of him. He clamped his hands around the cup as if he were afraid it might escape.

Roslyn was preparing the scrambled eggs, breaking the eggs into a bowl, adding milk, prattling away. "Mrs. Hopper must be excited about Terri coming home. It's been a while. I know I can't wait to see my kids when they've been away."

Nobody would ever mistake you for the all-knowing household help, Roslyn, he thought. He doubted if she realized that Evelyn and Terri weren't that close or that he and Evelyn had become strangers.

Detective Michel Brisbois leaned against a tree, tapping his pen against his notebook. He'd put on a suit fresh from the cleaners that morning but still managed to look rumpled. Detective Chester Creighton stood, hands in pockets, watching the forensics team work inside the yellow tape. He had the fresh, antiseptic look of a man who had just stepped from a *Rex Morgan, MD* comic strip.

"Let's go over this again," Brisbois said. "You were trundling a tray of pancakes and bacon up to the camp when you ran into Rudley."

Tim smiled. "Actually, it was popovers and sausages in citrus chutney."

Brisbois stared at him.

"Yes," said Tim.

"And then what?"

"I ran into Rudley. He was staggering toward the tent, looking as if someone had punched him in the midsection."

"And?"

"He said, 'We've got to call the police.' I followed him to the tent where Mrs. Rudley was rolling up the sleeping bags. She said, 'Rudley, what's wrong?' And he repeated, 'We've got to call the police.'"

Brisbois nodded. "What was his demeanour?"

"Shocked. Although I don't know why." Tim tittered, sobered as Brisbois frowned. "I asked what was wrong. He glared at me and said, 'There's a damned dead body back there.'"

"Then what?"

"Margaret gasped and said, 'Oh, no.' And Rudley said, 'Oh, yes.' And Margaret said, 'Are you sure he's dead?' And Rudley said, 'Clearly dead and it's not a he.' And Margaret said, 'Oh, no.'"

"And then?"

"Margaret and I went to the scene to confirm..." he paused, "well, you know."

"That the person was deceased."

"Yes," said Tim and hastened to add, "We didn't touch anything except to confirm she had no pulse. Her head was bashed in." He paused, blinked. "It was pretty awful. Rudley and I stayed with her while Margaret went down to call 911."

Brisbois flipped back through his notes. "Tell me again, what time did you come up here?"

Tim thought for a moment. "I brought the breakfast up a few minutes after I came on duty. So I must have run into Rudley around seven."

"And when did Rudley say he found the body?"

"Just before I ran into him."

Brisbois thought for a moment. "OK, Tim, you can go. We'll want to talk to you later." He wandered over to where Creighton was standing. "What's the word?"

"Doc thinks she's been dead six to ten hours," said Creighton. "She's got three head injuries, the big one at the base of the skull, a crease on the right, and a bump on the left. No obvious gunshot or stab wounds, no signs of strangulation. A few minor scrapes and abrasions on her hands and face." He consulted his notebook. "Off-white oxford-cloth shirt, designer jeans, black leather belt with a silver shamrock buckle. Ironic. Black leather half-Wellingtons. No ID."

Brisbois looked off into the trees. "She doesn't look too young."

"Doc thinks late forties."

"Good clothes. Looks as if she might have had some money."

Creighton nodded. "She's wearing a nice gold chain. Tan lines where she might have had a ring and watch."

"Think maybe they were stolen?"

"Could be."

Brisbois hitched up his pants. "You'd think a woman like that, if she went missing overnight, somebody might report it."

"Maybe she lived alone," said Creighton.

"You say she had no ID. Any keys?"

"Nope."

"If she lived alone you'd think she'd have some keys on her."

Creighton checked his notes. "There were a few coins in her right-hand pocket. Suggests she was right-handed. For all the good that does." He flipped the book shut. "Maybe whoever took the watch and ring took her wallet, got her address, took her keys, went back, and rifled her place."

Brisbois pushed back his hat. "We've got horseshoe prints all over the place.

"Maybe she fell off her horse and hit her head."

"Maybe."

Brisbois' gaze drifted over the scene. "So where's the horse?"

Creighton shrugged.

Brisbois pulled his cell phone out of his pocket. "Yes, I want to put out an APB on a horse." He listened. "No, I don't know what it looks like. Probably has a saddle. Check with Animal Control, the usual places." He paused. "I don't need that." He slammed the phone shut. Shoved it into his pocket. He had a dead woman on his hands, and the dispatcher was making jokes about a horse's ass. He turned to Creighton. "Have you got a team going door to door?"

"Petrie and Vance are on their way."

"OK." Brisbois started off down the hill. Creighton followed.

Brisbois settled into the chair behind Rudley's desk. Creighton sprawled on the settee, one leg over the arm.

"I'm glad you gentlemen feel so much at home," said Rudley.

Creighton swung his leg off the arm of the settee, sat forward, planting both feet on the floor.

"We appreciate your hospitality," said Brisbois.

"Yet again."

"Unfortunately." Brisbois opened his notebook. "I need to check some details."

Rudley folded his arms across his chest. "Yes?"

"You said you found the body when you got up to go to the bathroom. By bathroom, I presume you mean tree."

Rudley gave him a sour look. Brisbois waited him out.

"Actually, it was a shrub — nannyberry, I believe."

"And what time was that?"

"Around six-thirty."

"You said you literally tripped over the body."

"I tripped over a stump."

"And that's when you noticed the body?"

"Yes."

"Any sign of life?"

Rudley swallowed hard. "I'm afraid not."

"Before that, did you hear anything?"

"A woodpecker. Then a grosbeak."

"I meant during the night. Something happened to that woman a hundred and fifty yards from your campsite. You must have heard something."

Rudley scratched his head. "Something crashed through the underbrush at one point. Probably a deer. Margaret thought it was a bear. I'm sure it wasn't."

Brisbois made a note. "What time was that?"

"I'm not sure. Sometime after midnight. Perhaps later. I didn't look at my watch."

"Could it have been a horse?"

Rudley threw up his hands. "It could have been a zebra for all I know. It was dark. I woke from a sound sleep. I assumed it was a deer because there are quite a few up in the woods."

"OK," Brisbois murmured. "Did you hear anything else?"

"There was one thing or another scuttling around all night."

Brisbois waited, pen poised. "Do you know what time?"

"No. I was drifting in and out half the night."

"Anything that sounded like voices? Somebody having an argument?"

"No, nothing like that."

"OK, you tripped over the stump. You saw the woman's body. What did you do next?"

"I went to find Margaret."

"Did you move her? Check her pulse?"

"No. I could tell she was as dead as a doornail."

Brisbois raised his eyebrows. "Tim checked her pulse. I guess he wasn't as sure as you were."

Rudley glared.

"I know, I know," said Brisbois. "You've had more experience."

Brisbois spread a set of index cards out on the desk, studied them for a few minutes. "So what do we have here?"

Creighton ran a hand through his hair. "The children were sleeping all snug in their beds. Ma and Pa were in a tent in the woods. Nobody saw or heard anything, except Geraldine Phipps-Walker, who heard a nighthawk. Which is not a true hawk, mind you, but a member of the nightjar family."

"Spare me."

"Just being thorough, Boss."

Brisbois shook his head, picked up an index card. "Norman Phipps-Walker and Mr. Tee Lawrence took a night fishing charter from the dock in Middleton. Lloyd drove them in and picked them up near eleven. Norman went straight to his room — where I'm sure his wife entertained him with details of that nightjar thing. Lawrence went to his cabin. Neither of them noticed anything unusual. Mr. James Bole was up at the inn until nearly eleven. He took part in a games night and put on a puppet show. *Waiting for Godot.*" He frowned. "What in hell is that?"

"Beats me."

"The Sawchucks took part in the Snakes and Ladders tournament. They went to bed around ten. Neither of them saw or heard anything." Brisbois put the card aside, picked up another. "Mr. Carty. Who's that again?"

"Rico. The young guy at the Oaks."

"Oh, yeah. He had dinner, spent the evening in his cabin, watching the Blue Jays game. Turned out the lights as soon as the game was over. Kind of early for a young kid."

"He said he'd been working a lot of overtime."

Brisbois rubbed his chin. "Still, seems kind of funny. Young guy, works at the racetrack in Ottawa, takes classes at Carleton. I wonder where he got the money to come here."

"Maybe from all that overtime."

Brisbois shrugged. "Still, seems like a funny place for a young guy to take a vacation. You'd think if he wanted to fish, he'd get a bunch of his buddies and go camping."

"Is that what you did when you were his age?"

"I was married when I was his age. Mary and I went to Niagara Falls. We went down east the next couple of years. Then we had a baby on the way. Then we had four. Neither of us has had a real vacation since." Brisbois wrote a note on the index card, put it aside. "Where'd you go on your last trip? Myrtle Beach, wasn't it?"

"Yup."

"Miss Miller and Mr. Simpson," said Brisbois, drawing out another card.

Creighton chuckled. "Miss Miller's been kind of quiet so far. Seems strange not having her in the middle of everything. Although, I'm sure she will be."

"Although I'm sure she will be," Brisbois murmured. "Miss Miller and Mr. Simpson were at the inn all evening. In Margaret and Rudley's absence, they were overseeing games night. Snakes and Ladders and canasta."

"Aren't they those clicking things the flamenco dancers use?"

"I don't think so." Brisbois checked another index card. "The Lawrences, Bonnie and Tee. What does the T stand for?"

"Nothing. That's his name. Tee James Lawrence. T-e-e. It's his mother's maiden name."

"He was on the fishing charter with Norman," Brisbois murmured. "Bonnie Lawrence had dinner in the dining room with Geraldine, then retired to her cabin, and spent the rest of the evening planning Miss Miller's wedding."

"Does it take that long?"

Brisbois gave him a long look. "Believe me, it can take months."

Creighton grinned. "Well, I can't wait to find out where they're going to have it. So far, I've heard it might be in the woods, or in a canoe on the lake. I heard one rumour they might tie the knot in goggles and flippers."

"I think that's just a rumour. OK" — Brisbois took out another index card — "the Benson sisters. They were watching a James Cagney marathon. They didn't hear a thing."

"Are they still alive?"

"So they say." Brisbois closed his notebook, put it into his pocket, stacked the index cards, put them into the desk drawer and locked it. "Maybe Mr. Arnold's slept it off by now."

"I'll bet he doesn't remember anything."

"It's worth a try," Brisbois said, "if only for the satisfaction of waking him up."

Chapter 5

"Where did you find him, Lloyd?" Margaret reached to stroke the handsome black horse.

"He came into the garden where I was hoeing. Nice as you please."

"He seems very gentle."

"Like a lamb. Name's Ned. Says on his bridle."

Margaret's eyes fell on the horse's shoulder. "My goodness, he's got a nasty gash there."

Lloyd nodded. "Must have got into the brambles. Had blood all down his shoulder and onto his leg. He was dirty, too, and full of burrs. I washed him down."

"That was very kind of you." Margaret smoothed the horse's mane. "He must belong to someone near here."

"Don't know."

"I'll call Animal Control," Margaret said. "Someone must be looking for him."

Creighton hammered at the door to the Pines. Brisbois stood by, hands in pockets.

Creighton massaged his knuckles. "This is like trying to wake the dead." He tried the door. "It isn't locked." He turned to Brisbois, grinned. "Did you hear somebody say 'come in'?"

Brisbois nodded. "Yeah, I think I did."

Creighton pushed open the door. "Mr. Arnold?"

Arnold lay sprawled across the bed on his abdomen.

"Mr. Arnold. Police."

No response.

Brisbois glanced around. "The place looks as if a tornado hit it."

Creighton pointed to a pair of pants, halfway across the room. "He's got mud up to his knees. He must have crawled home."

Brisbois gestured toward the bed. "Let's make sure he's OK."

Creighton snickered. "Blue boxer shorts with little white clouds."

"Cloud 9," said Brisbois.

"You've got to be kidding."

"That's what it says." Brisbois leaned over the bed. "Mr. Arnold." He grabbed him by the shoulder, gave it a vigorous shake. "Sir, wake up."

Arnold groaned, turned over, opened one eye.

Brisbois produced his badge. "Police."

Arnold blinked.

"Sit up, please." Brisbois turned to Creighton. "Could you get him a glass of water?"

"Over the head, I hope." Creighton found a mug on the table. He took it to the sink, filled it with water. He returned, handed the mug to Arnold.

Arnold took a swig, spluttered. "This tastes like piss."

"Sorry," said Creighton. "I guess I didn't let the tap run long enough."

Brisbois pulled up a chair, sat down. "Do you mind answering a few questions?"

Arnold shoved his hair out of his eyes. "This had better be good. I had a lousy night."

"Oh, it's good," said Brisbois.

Arnold gave him a wary look.

"Where were you last night?"

Arnold ran a hand across his chest, coughed. "I went into town."

"What time?"

"I don't know exactly. Sometime after supper. Around dusk."

"Notice anything unusual? Anybody on the road?"

Arnold looked at him as if he were crazy. "There was the odd car."

Brisbois turned a page in his notebook. "OK, where'd you go in town?"

"The hotel."

"What time did you get back?"

Arnold hesitated. "I don't know. Late, I guess."

Brisbois stared at Arnold for a long moment. "How'd you get home?"

Arnold squinted. "I drove."

Brisbois raised his brows. "I heard they found you sacked out on the veranda this morning, smelling like a distillery."

Arnold snorted. "They sent two detectives out here over a DUI?"

Brisbois glanced at Creighton. "We're a small detachment. We — what is it you call it? — multitask."

Arnold took a deep breath, looked around. "Look guys, I figured I wasn't in any shape to drive, so I pulled over."

"Commendable," Brisbois said. "So you walked home?"

"Yeah. So you guys came for nothing. No DUI."

Brisbois ignored this. "How far did you walk?"

Arnold drew a hand through his hair. "From where I left my car."

"And how far would that be?"

"I don't know exactly. How can you tell out here?"

Brisbois watched him for a moment. "Your pants" — he gestured toward the crumpled trousers — "how did they get so dirty?"

"I took a shortcut."

"Through a mud puddle?"

"No, through that boggy area." Arnold paused as Brisbois stared. "Hey, it was messy but it was short. Else, I'd have had to go all the way around on the road."

Brisbois smiled. "And you didn't want to get caught beside your car, ten times over the limit."

Arnold looked hurt. "Hey, I was a little wobbly. If I'd stayed on the road, I might have been hit by a car."

Brisbois rolled his eyes. "You had to be a pretty good navigator to find your way back to the Pleasant through the swamp."

Arnold smirked. "I went as true as the crow flies. I came out right into the driveway."

"Amazing. In the dark. In an unfamiliar place."

Arnold shrugged. "I'm a builder. I have good spatial sense."

Too bad you don't have any other kind of sense, Brisbois thought. "So what time did you get back?" he said.

Arnold looked into the cup, swished the water around. "Look, can you get me something from the fridge? Maybe a Coke."

Creighton spun off the wall, returned with a can of ginger ale. He opened it, shoved it into Arnold's hand.

Arnold took a long drink.

"What time?" Brisbois prompted.

"I don't know." Arnold looked to Brisbois, found only a riveting stare. "Late." He paused, studied their faces. "This isn't about a DUI."

Brisbois shook his head.

Arnold dragged his hand across his mouth. "It's about that dame in the bar, isn't it? I'll bet she claimed I was harassing her."

Brisbois didn't respond.

"Look, all I did was ask her to have a drink with me. Ask the bartender. I didn't touch her."

"Did you catch this woman's name?"

Arnold snorted. "We didn't get that far."

Brisbois scribbled some notes. "So you had a confrontation with a woman in the bar. Then what?"

Arnold shrugged. "Nothing. I hung around the bar, had a few more drinks, then I came home."

"What happened to the woman?"

Arnold stared at him. "How in hell should I know? She threw a drink in my face and stormed out."

"OK." Brisbois flipped a page. "So you left the bar and started home. Did you see anything?"

Arnold shook his head. "Hell, I can't remember. There might have been a car or two, but I don't remember anything in particular." He paused, took a drink. "What's this about, anyway?"

Brisbois sat back, let the silence build for a minute. "We found a body. Might have been near where you were."

Arnold's jaw dropped. "You think I killed somebody? You're crazy."

Brisbois glanced at Creighton. "We're just asking questions." He gestured toward the trousers. "We'd like to take your pants, have a look at them, if you're agreeable."

"Are you charging me with something?"

"No, just asking for your cooperation."

Arnold stared at him for a moment. "Take whatever you want. I didn't kill anybody." His lips parted in a sloppy grin. "I'm a lover, not a fighter."

Brisbois stood. "Thank you for your cooperation."

Arnold waved this off. "No problem, buddy. I've got nothing to hide."

"That's good."

Arnold reached for a tumbler and a bottle of whisky on the bedside table. "Oh, by the way…"

"Yes?"

"Could you get those pants cleaned before you bring them back?"

Terri Hopper arrived home around eleven. Roslyn had just finished washing the kitchen floor. Terri stopped a few feet inside the door. "Sorry, Ros."

"It's OK, honey, it's just about dry."

Terri took off her shoes, tiptoed in, looked around. "Where's Dad?"

"He went upstairs to have a shower a while ago. Maybe he fell asleep. He took a couple of pills for his tooth before he went up."

"How did the dentist go yesterday?"

Roslyn moved the mop pail to one side. "I think he had kind of a rough day. The pills they gave him made him all fluey. He said he fell.

When I got here, I thought he'd been rolling in Drummie's dirt pile. He looked like that kid from the Charlie Brown comic."

"Pig Pen?"

"Yeah, that's the one. He said he slept on the couch. I don't know if he had any supper. I made him some scrambled eggs. He hardly touched them."

Terri frowned. "Where's Mom?"

"Your dad said she went riding." Roslyn glanced at the clock. "Gosh, she's been gone a while. She was away when I got here." She paused. "Do you want me to fix you some lunch?"

Terri gave her a hug. "Oh, no thanks, Ros. I stopped for something on the way. I'll just go up and look in on Dad."

Roslyn went on with her cleaning. Terri went upstairs. The door to the master bedroom was ajar. She knocked, peeked in.

Carl lay on the bed in his bathrobe, fast asleep, his hair still damp from the shower.

"I'll be back in a few minutes, Dad," she whispered.

She ran back downstairs, grabbed some carrots from the kitchen, called to Roslyn as she passed the living room, "Ros, I'm going down to see the horses."

She hurried down the path to the stable. She was worried about her father, and it wasn't just because he'd had a lousy day at the dentist and ended up sleeping on the couch. He looked so thin. He would never tell her, but she knew his depression was getting worse. He was having trouble with the latest manuscript. He'd told her it was nothing — just a temporary block — but she knew the deadline was a pressure he didn't need.

Her mother wasn't much help. She couldn't even be bothered to look after him after the dental appointment. She knew her dad was a baby about things like that, but at least her mother could have made sure he was all right before she left.

She went into the stable, almost tripped over a shovel lying a few feet inside the door. She propped it against the wall and went to check the horses. Gert neighed. Maisie tossed her head. Bob grabbed at her sleeve. She gave them the carrots.

Ned's stall was empty.

She walked back up the line. None of the stalls had been mucked out. It wasn't like her mother to go riding without cleaning the stalls, or, at least, turning the horses out into the paddock. She went to get the shovel, uttered an exclamation of disgust as she noticed the gelatinous streaks down the blade. Maybe one of the horses had stomped a mouse, she thought. She took the shovel outside, hosed it down, and leaned it against the wall to dry. She released the horses into the paddock and went back inside. She took the pitchfork down from the wall, headed toward the stalls, stopped as a glint of silver caught her eye. She bent and picked up her father's glasses. What were they doing here? She hung the pitchfork back on the wall and ran up to the house.

Terri heard the whine of the vacuum cleaner from the dining room as she entered the house. Roslyn's not unpleasant voice broke occasionally over the whir. She went upstairs.

Carl Hopper hadn't moved. Terri picked up the clothes he had left on the floor at the foot of the bed and headed toward the laundry hamper in the en suite. She opened the lid, preparing to drop them in, frowned. Roslyn was right. The clothes did look as if he'd been rolling in a dirt pile. She stared at the straw ground into the knees of his jeans. More like rolling around in a stable, she thought. The shirt was dirty and stained with what could have been horse manure. She folded the clothes, placed them on the lid of the hamper, and went back into the bedroom.

"Dad?"

His eyelids fluttered.

"Dad, it's Terri."

He smiled drunkenly without opening his eyes.

She shook him by the shoulder. "Dad, wake up."

He opened his eyes.

"Were you in the barn this morning?"

He looked at her as if she had asked him to recite the BNA Act.

"What happened to your clothes?"

He closed his eyes.

"Dad, I found your glasses." They felt sweaty in her hand.

He gave her a goofy smile. "Thanks."

He started to turn over. She stopped him with a hand on his shoulder. "Dad, did you and Mom have a fight?"

He frowned.

"The stable's a mess," she persisted. "She hasn't mucked out the stalls. She didn't even turn the horses out. I don't even know if she fed them." She bent so she was looking directly into his eyes. "Did Mom go off in a huff?"

"I don't..." He closed his eyes, frowning as if struggling to find the answer. "'bout what?" he muttered and fell asleep.

She surmised the pills he'd taken were in no danger of wearing off imminently. "Damned if I know, Dad."

Tim rolled a trolley out onto the veranda. "Lunch is served." He placed a club sandwich in front of Miss Miller. Fish and chips for Simpson.

"Anything new to report?" asked Miss Miller.

"The police took something out of Mr. Arnold's cabin."

Miss Miller leaned forward. "Do they think he's the culprit?"

Tim shrugged. "I suspect they're curious about what he was doing passed out on the veranda at six a.m., covered with mud."

"Interesting."

"Although, if they asked for my opinion, I'd say he was probably too drunk to do much."

"Has the victim been identified?"

"Not as far as we know."

Simpson frowned. "Terrible thing. I wonder why someone would be out in the woods at that time of night."

"We don't know."

"Are they sure she was murdered during the night?"

"That's the word, Miss Miller."

Miss Miller thought for a moment. "Perhaps she didn't intend to be in the woods. Perhaps she was kidnapped. Or murdered elsewhere and left in the woods."

"I don't know, Miss Miller. The information is coming in slowly."

"Meaning Officer Owens isn't in the loop yet."

"It's his day off." Tim paused to acknowledge Doreen Sawchuck, who was waving frantically. "Excuse me. Mrs. Sawchuck needs her lunch so she can take her pills."

Miss Miller watched Tim walk away.

Simpson cleared his throat. "Elizabeth, I hope you're not planning to get involved in any of this."

She gave him an innocent look.

"We have to focus on the wedding. We have some details to tidy up." She smiled. "Edward, would I think of getting involved?"

"Of course, you would."

Bonnie and Tee Lawrence came up the steps to the veranda at that moment. Bonnie looked flushed.

"I came up with some wonderful ideas for the wedding," Bonnie said. "I had everything written down and forgot to bring the notes. That awful thing that happened…"

Tee looked somber. "Terrible," he said.

"I hope it won't interfere with the wedding," Bonnie fretted.

"We appreciate your efforts," said Simpson, "but we don't want you to worry yourself."

Bonnie sighed. "We can't have something like that interfering with the wedding."

Tee looked irritated. "The wedding will turn out fine, Bonnie, whether you fuss about it or not."

She looked at him, hurt. He took her arm and steered her into the inn.

"Mrs. Lawrence seems quite distressed," Simpson said.

"Mrs. Lawrence is brainless."

"That's terribly elitist of you, Elizabeth. I'm sure Mrs. Lawrence is gifted in her own way."

She took his hand. "You're such a sweet person. Always wanting to see good in everyone."

"My parents taught me there's something good to be said for everyone."

"I'm not sure about that. What sort of person would bludgeon a woman to death?"

He gave her a long look. "The sort of person we'd best avoid."

She smiled. "Of course, Edward."

Brisbois put his hand over the phone, turned to Creighton. "Petrie and Vance came across Arnold's car." He turned back to the phone. "OK. Thanks. Secure the site. It could be part of a crime scene." He slipped the phone into his pocket. "That idiot Arnold drove his car into the ditch up in the woods. Petrie says the driver's door was open. His wallet was on the floor. He must have been some drunk." He took out his notebook. "I'm surprised he found his way back to the inn — even with his great spatial sense."

Creighton smiled. "He leaves the car in the ditch and sets out cross-country, right through that boggy area east of the inn. Just as he said."

Brisbois cocked an index finger at him. "It would also bring him kind of close to where that woman was found." He jammed his hands into his pockets. "Or maybe he wandered into her bailiwick and the rest is history."

Creighton shrugged. "From the way he looked, I don't know if he would have had the wherewithal to kill her."

Brisbois thought for a moment. "He may not have had the coordination to drive, but I'll bet he had enough strength to commit murder. He was mad. A woman had just insulted him in a bar. Maybe the same woman." He paused. "You think maybe we've got probable cause for a warrant?"

Creighton grinned. "I think we do."

Rudley ran down the front steps as the laundryman pulled up in front of the Pleasant, accosting the man as he got down from his truck. "You're late."

"I am not late, Mr. Rudley. I was detained."

Rudley crossed his eyes.

"I suffered a mechanical malfunction."

"I've been keeping an eye out for you all morning. I wanted to make sure I caught you. Those serviettes you brought yesterday aren't the right ones."

The laundryman went to the back of the truck, loaded his dolly. "We have your order under control, Mrs. Rudley and I."

"You spoke to Margaret?"

"I did. Mrs. Rudley has kept me constantly apprised of the latest requirements for your fête." He looked at Rudley over his glasses. "Don't you speak to Mrs. Rudley?"

"Now, see here."

"If you had spoken to Mrs. Rudley," the laundryman went on, impervious to Rudley's glare, "you would have known that the napkins for the wedding will be delivered on the morning of the wedding. The napkins delivered yesterday were replacements for those of general use that have become discoloured, frayed, or have otherwise been rendered unsuitable for your fine establishment and exacting standards." As Rudley began to splutter, he added, "I wouldn't feel too badly, Rudley. A wedding in the family is always a disorienting experience." He wheeled the dolly around smartly and headed for the back entrance before Rudley could respond.

Rudley charged back up the steps into the lobby.

Margaret was on the phone, brow furrowed as she listened. "Oh, dear. I see," she said finally. "Well, thank you." She hung up.

"What's the matter, Margaret?"

"The Reverend Burley in Brockton is not available to perform the ceremony. Apparently, he made an error in his booking schedule. He's on vacation in Ireland and won't return until after the date."

"They must have someone to fill in."

"June's a popular month for weddings, Rudley. His replacement already has three weddings on that day. The secretary suggested Miss Miller might try to get someone from her home parish."

"No need for that, Margaret. We can get that old guy from Middleton to fill in."

"Reverend Pendergast? I believe he's retired."

"Men of the cloth don't retire."

"I've heard he's a little forgetful."

"I can't see how that would be a problem. There are enough of us here who've been through the ceremony. If he stumbles, someone will cue him."

She didn't look convinced.

"I could perform a wedding in my sleep," Rudley went on. "I can't see why innkeepers can't marry people when all sorts of ninnies are allowed to."

"I believe all those *ninnies* have to have been invested with the authority, Rudley."

"Yes," he fumed, "some blockhead clerk can marry a couple, while a man of sensibilities cannot." Rudley paused, gave Margaret a jaunty smile. "What the hell. A wedding is a wonderful thing."

"It is." She gave him a peck on the cheek. "I'm so glad to see you in good spirits."

"When am I not?"

"I have to check on something in the kitchen," she said.

He whistled a few bars of "Get Me to the Church on Time" and did a little shuffle. Why shouldn't he be in good spirits? He regretted the fate of the woman in the forest as he regretted the passing of any person. But the murder hadn't taken place at the Pleasant proper and didn't involve anyone on the premises. Still, terrible thing to kill a woman. "Although, I have been sorely tempted at times," he murmured as Mrs. Sawchuck hobbled into the lobby. The woman's death was a tragedy, but they had to do their best not to let the murder put a damper on the wedding. At least they had the worst out of the way. He was sure everything would go smoothly from there on in. The Reverend Pendergast would be quite satisfactory, probably much better than that fellow from Brockton with his baby face and pale-grey getup. Give me a mature man in black any day, he thought. One who knows the meaning of the vows. These young pups presiding over weddings these days know half of them will end in divorce and they conduct the ceremony accordingly. He deplored the climbing divorce rate. People marrying willy-nilly, based on whim, then dropping the whole thing when they no longer felt entertained. Time was, you married for life and you stuck it out, however unpleasant the situation. Marriage was a test of character, a test of fortitude — like a slog to the South Pole.

Margaret returned from the kitchen with a tray. "Rudley, you haven't had your lunch. Gregoire's coleslaw is divine today."

"Thank you, Margaret."

The phone rang. Margaret answered. "You don't say. Thank you." She glanced out the window, brightened. "Excuse me." She took off down the steps.

He smiled. "Now, there's a woman who's worth a slog to the South Pole."

Brisbois and Creighton were headed across the lawn. Margaret called to them. "Detectives."

They turned.

She hurried toward them. "I just got a call from Animal Control. They said you were looking for a horse."

They looked at her, bewildered.

"Well, we found him." She took Brisbois by the arm, hurried him toward the coach house. "Or, rather, he found us. You see, Lloyd was working in the garden, and he just walked in. We called Animal Control. We assumed he belonged to someone near here. We assumed someone would be looking for him, then a gentleman just called to say the police wanted him." She stopped at the coach house where Lloyd was putting down a bucket for water for the horse.

"Nice-looking animal." Brisbois gave the horse a long look. He turned to Lloyd. "What time did he come into the garden?"

"Early." Lloyd gave the horse a pat. "Says his name's Ned."

Creighton chuckled. "I wouldn't believe anything a horse told me."

Margaret gave Creighton a reproachful look.

"Ned," Lloyd repeated. "Says so on his bridle."

Brisbois took out his phone. "Yeah, Brisbois here. I need someone to come down to the Pleasant. I've got the horse."

The forensics officer grinned. "This guy's the cleanest crime scene I've been at."

Brisbois glowered. "Lloyd cleaned him up. Can you get anything?"

"I think so." He pointed to the mane. "Look at this. A couple of strands of matted hair. Our man missed them when he gave him his shower."

"Blood?"

"Probably. We'll know shortly." The officer tapped Ned on the leg. Ned obliged by lifting his foot. "His forelegs are as clean as a whistle, but there's lots of good stuff in his shoes." He looked at Brisbois. "You think the horse is the killer? He doesn't seem the type."

"You're a real card, Sheffield."

Sheffield stood, pointed to the horse's shoulder. "This is interesting. The area around the wound's been cleaned up but, right in the centre, there's guess what?"

"Pearls of wisdom, I hope, since all I've been getting all morning are bad horse jokes."

Sheffield grinned. "Almost as good. Some little bits of chaff, one recognizable husk, and a strand of thick white hair which clearly isn't his."

"Human?"

"No, it's pretty coarse. Probably another horse. Maybe a cow."

"Hm." Brisbois rocked back on his heels. "So he hangs out on a farm. He gets cut, rolls in the straw, picks up this stuff."

"Maybe. Although you'd think he'd have some stuck in his mane." Sheffield shrugged. "Of course, your man Lloyd could have brushed it out."

"And what did he get cut with?" Brisbois murmured. His phone rang. He groped in his pocket for it. "Brisbois." He listened, taking notes. "Thanks." He turned to Creighton. "That was the morgue. They think they know who our Jane Doe is."

Chapter 6

Terri Hopper was coming out of the stable when the unfamiliar car pulled into the driveway. She watched as two men got out, one tall and angular with a felt hat tipped over his eyes. He reminded her of Eliot Ness. The other reminded her of her history professor, the frumpy Mr. Taylor. The men exchanged a few words, then went up to the house. She waited a few minutes, then followed.

Fragments of conversation drifted to her from the kitchen as she eased the front door open. Eliot Ness leaned against the kitchen door jamb, his back to her. She guessed the unfamiliar voice belonged to Professor Taylor.

The floorboards creaked as she crept forward to listen. Eliot Ness straightened, glanced over his shoulder at her but said nothing. He stepped aside as she approached the door.

Her father sat at the table, still in his robe, his face slack. Roslyn stood, her back pressed against the counter, fingers clutching the edge.

The chunky man looked up, then turned to Carl and said in a low voice, "Is this your daughter?"

Her father looked at her as if he'd never seen her before.

She stepped forward. "Yes, I'm Terri."

He stood. "Terri, I'm Detective Brisbois."

"Detective Creighton," the tall man said.

"There's been an accident," Brisbois said.

Roslyn started to sob. "It's your mother, Terri. They found her up in the woods."

"I'm afraid…" Brisbois began.

Terri's breath caught in her throat. "She's dead, isn't she?"

He nodded. "I'm sorry. A technician at the hospital made a tentative identification. We'll need someone to confirm it's her."

She hesitated.

He looked to Carl. "Is there someone?"

The tip of Carl's tongue lolled to one corner of his mouth. A drop of saliva fell on the table in front of him.

"Aunt Joan," Terri said. "Joan Metcalfe."

Brisbois offered her his cell phone. "If you'd like to call her, we can pick her up on our way to the hospital." He put a hand on her shoulder as she hesitated. "Would you like me to do it?"

"How?" she said.

"We're not sure yet. She may have fallen off her horse."

"Ned? Have you found him?"

"Yes. He wandered onto a neighbour's property."

"Is he all right?"

He studied her face. "He's OK. They took good care of him."

Carl uttered a guttural sound.

Brisbois lowered his voice. "Does your father have health problems?"

She hesitated. "He's had some problems."

"Heart?"

She shook her head.

"It looks as if he's a little hung over."

"He took some pills. Codeine. The dentist gave it to him. He's not good with things like that."

"OK." Brisbois turned back to Carl Hopper. "Sir, are you able to come with us in the car?"

Carl stared at him.

Roslyn mopped her face with the end of her apron. "I'll get him some clothes."

"Thanks." Brisbois turned to Creighton, said in a low voice,

"Let's give the ladies a hand getting him dressed. Doesn't look as if he's up to much."

Brisbois drove to the hospital. Creighton sat in the passenger seat, glancing periodically into the rear-view mirror.

"We might have to drop him off at emergency," Creighton said.

Brisbois took a quick look. Carl Hopper sagged against the window, eyes glazed. Mrs. Joan Metcalfe, an angular older woman with a wind-burned face and good dye job, sat in the middle, clutching Terri's hand. Terri stared out the window, nibbling on a thumbnail.

Brisbois grimaced. Carl Hopper struck him as self-indulgent. He knew if anything happened to Mary, he'd be devastated. Still, he believed he'd be able to summon the strength to comfort their children. This man had barely looked at his daughter. He could read the distress in Mrs. Metcalfe's eyes, but she was clearly determined to remain calm for the girl's sake.

They reached the hospital. Brisbois pulled up to the emergency entrance. Creighton hopped out to open the door for the women. Brisbois opened the door to help Carl out. Carl sat still, staring at the back of the seat.

Brisbois leaned into the car. "Mr. Hopper?" Receiving no response, he took the man by the arm and guided him out of the car.

The elevator took them to the morgue. Brisbois spoke to the attendant, then returned and said in a low voice, "They'll just open the curtain." He guided them to the viewing area.

After a few minutes, the curtain opened.

Mrs. Metcalfe nodded, grabbed a swath of Kleenex from her purse, dabbed at her eyes, then stuffed the Kleenex into her pocket as if they had shamed her.

Terri took a long look. "It's Mom," she whispered.

Carl Hopper fainted.

"I know this is tough." Brisbois sat on a straight-back chair in the quiet room, leaning toward Terri, who sat on the couch opposite.

Creighton stood by the window, the curtain pushed aside with one finger, staring at the hospital parking lot.

"I should check on Dad."

Brisbois held up a hand. "Your dad's going to be OK. He passed out."

She bit her lip. "He can't handle things like this. He's been depressed."

"For a long time?"

"Mostly this last year. He's been under a lot of pressure."

"Pressure?"

"He has a contract. He's been having trouble with a manuscript."

"Your dad's a writer?"

She nodded. "He writes science fiction under the name T.R. Reilly."

Brisbois made a note, balancing the notebook against his thigh. "What about your mother? Were she and your dad having problems?"

She took a deep breath. "A little, I guess."

"Did they fight a lot?"

"No." She paused. "Mostly Mom just got nasty. Dad took it. He never fought back."

He didn't take his eyes off her. "What did they fight about?"

She shook her head. "The pills. The doctor ordered antidepressants. Mom didn't think he should be taking them."

He made a note. "So they fought about the pills. Anything else?"

"No."

He waited her out.

She inhaled sharply. "I know what you're thinking. You think Dad did something to Mom. That's impossible." She looked away. "You don't even know what happened."

He looked at her for a long moment. "This is routine, Terri."

She said nothing.

He gave her a few minutes, then said. "Can you think of anybody who'd want to hurt your mother?"

"No."

"What did she do?"

"She was an interior decorator. She had her own business."

"What about co-workers?"

"She didn't have any. She worked on her own."

"Were most of her clients local?"

"No, she had clients everywhere." She shook her head. "I'm sorry. I don't know very much about her work."

"Do you live at home?"

"No, I'm working in Ottawa for the summer. I'm still in school."

"Ottawa U.?"

"Carleton. I just came home today. I'm taking a week off."

"Do you know any of her friends, clients?"

"Aunt Joan. She's not really an aunt. She's a friend of Mom's." She paused. "You might as well know. Mom and I weren't that close. We didn't talk that much."

"Didn't get along?"

"Not really."

"What did you not get along about?"

"Nothing in particular. We just didn't have much in common."

He thought about that for a minute. "What about your dad? Did you talk to him?"

"Sure."

He waited.

"We talked about what we were doing. About my courses. Dad was really interested in what I was doing at school."

"Did your mom travel in her work?"

"Yes."

"Did your dad go with her?"

"No."

"Did she have mostly private clients? Commercial?"

"Both. Not big commercial. Offices. Dad said she sometimes designed reception areas."

He made some notes. "So you and your mother weren't close."

"No."

He held her gaze. "The coroner thinks your mother died around midnight. What would she have been doing, riding at that time of night?"

She shrugged. "Mom loved the horses. If she was trying to relax, or think something through, she'd take Ned up the laneway, maybe a little ways down the road, or she might just walk him around the paddock."

"Up into the woods?"

Terri shook her head. "No, Mom would never go up into the woods at night."

"But that's where she ended up."

"She'd never take Ned up into the woods. Especially not at night. She'd worry about him stepping into a hole."

"OK." He scribbled a note. "Can you think of anybody she might have had a quarrel with recently? Over property lines and so forth?"

"No, I don't think there was anything like that. Dad would have told me."

"So, you go to university in Ottawa."

"Yes."

"When did you get home?"

"This morning."

"Bus? Train?"

"I drove."

"OK," he said half to himself. "So you weren't expecting her to pick you up. When did you last talk to her?"

"A couple of weeks ago."

"She call you or did you call her?"

"I called home. Mom answered the phone."

He looked up, surprised, then returned to his notes. When he looked up again, Terri was wiping away tears.

"Can I go now? I really should check to see if Dad needs anything. And I left the horses in the paddock. I forgot to check the latch. We left in such a hurry."

He thought for a moment. "OK, that's enough for now. We'll probably want to talk to you later."

She scrambled up, like a kid released from the principal's office. "Would you tell Aunt Joan I'll give her a call?"

He smiled. "Sure." He waited until she left the room, then turned to Creighton. "What do you think?"

Creighton turned away from the window. "I think she likes her father better than her mother."

"Yeah, she pretty much said that."

Creighton sat down on the couch. "The antidepressants seemed to be a big deal at home. I wonder how Evelyn liked old Carl taking codeine."

Brisbois studied his notes, looked up with a smile. "I'd guess not very much."

Joan Metcalfe took the seat Terri had vacated a few minutes earlier. Brisbois drew a line under his interview with Terri, wrote down the date, time, and the particulars of the lady who sat opposite him.

"I'm sorry to bother you with this at this time, Mrs. Metcalfe, but the sooner we get some information, the better."

She nodded. "I understand."

"OK." Brisbois gave her an encouraging smile. "How long have you known Evelyn Hopper?"

"For about ten years. She was living in Brockton when I first met her. She boarded Gert and Maisie, her horses, with me. She came out two or three times a week to ride, sometimes just to visit the horses."

"Was she married to Carl Hopper then?"

She looked startled. "Of course. Terri is…"

"It was a first marriage for both of them?"

"Yes. Evelyn and Carl have been married almost twenty-five years."

"So she boarded horses with you, then she moved out here."

"Yes."

"So she and Carl came out here to raise horses."

She shook her head. "Oh, no, the horses weren't a business. After they moved out here, Evelyn continued to work as she always had. Carl did retire from his job. He was in advertising in the city. He decided to try his hand at writing fiction."

"Is he any good?"

She paused. "I don't read that sort of thing. He writes mainly science fiction. But, by all accounts, he did quite well."

He studied her for a moment. "Is he a drinker?"

"Not to excess."

"His daughter said he was depressed."

"Yes."

"Do you know what he was depressed about?"

She shook her head. "Not really. I think he's just one of those people who has a tendency toward depression."

"Did the depression cause problems in the marriage?"

She sighed. "I don't see how it couldn't cause some problems, Detective."

He paused. "Such as?"

She set her jaw. "I don't want my words to be misconstrued, Detective. Carl is a gentle sort of man. There was no abusive behaviour in the marriage. But I think his mental state made him seem weak, ineffectual. Evelyn didn't tolerate that well in a man — in anyone, for that matter."

"Were there money troubles?"

She looked at him as if he had asked her to describe her sex life. "I believe they were doing well. Her business was thriving. He was reasonably successful. Investment income, you know, the usual."

He smiled at that. "Even though he had psychiatric problems."

She thought for a moment. "Carl managed his depression quite well until recently. He'd hit a rough patch, but I believe he would have worked his way through that in time."

"But Evelyn wasn't too sympathetic?"

She shook her head. "As I've said, Evelyn had no patience for what she perceived to be weakness. And she wasn't particularly supportive of his writing career. I don't think she thought it was a fit pursuit for a man."

He made a note. "These tensions in the marriage, were they recent?"

She sighed. "No, I think they had existed for some time. I think they were gradually becoming less involved in one another's lives. Evelyn didn't resent or hate Carl. I think he simply ceased to be part of her plans."

"Did Carl feel the same way?"

"No," she said without hesitation. "Carl worshipped Evelyn."

"Do you know if they ever talked about divorce, saw a counselor, anything like that?"

She smiled slightly. "Oh, Evelyn wouldn't do anything like that. If she made up her mind to cut someone out of her life, that would be that."

Brisbois glanced at Creighton, then back at Joan. "Do you think he killed her?"

"No."

"You seem very sure about that."

"I am."

"People do strange things in the heat of passion."

She considered this. "I don't think Carl has the energy for passion."

He regarded her evenly. "Maybe that was the problem." He scribbled a half-page of notes. "So you and Evelyn became friends because of the horses. Did you have any other contact with her?"

"Oh, yes, Evelyn and I shared quite a few interests. Horses, horticulture, architecture. Her parents died young. I think I was a mother figure."

Brisbois nodded. He could see this solid woman as a mother figure. "Mrs. Metcalfe, you're saying Evelyn and Carl had grown apart. But they were married for twenty-five years. How much of that was a charade?"

She frowned. "You have to remember, Detective, Evelyn was young when she met Carl. He had been out of university for some time. He had a good job, was well-regarded in his field. At one time, he had plans to open his own agency. I'm sure Evelyn saw him as a real go-getter in those days. As she matured, I think she became more aware of his flaws. That often happens when women come into their own. I think her disillusionment was probably complete by the time they moved out here."

"And Carl gave up his business to write."

"Yes."

"Did they fight about that?"

"Evelyn wouldn't waste her time fighting about something she wasn't interested in. Carl wouldn't fight at all. It wasn't in him to be assertive, let alone aggressive. That's why I'm so sure he didn't harm Evelyn. And he loved her."

"But she didn't love him."

"Not in the way he would have liked, I'm sure."

"Was she having an affair?"

He expected her to take umbrage. Instead she merely looked thoughtful. "I have no idea," she said finally.

Her reaction caught him off guard. "Wouldn't she have told you?"

She smiled. "Evelyn wasn't the gossipy type. Most of what I've told you about her relationship with Carl is based on observation coupled with my sense of her general view on life. There was nothing schoolgirlish about her."

He tried a different approach. "Was there anything in her behaviour that might make you think something was going on? Was she moody? Distracted?"

She thought for a moment. "Evelyn could be moody and distracted at times. That was the way she was. But, no, nothing that struck me as unusual."

He rubbed his forehead. "Can you think of anyone she might have had a problem with?"

"Evelyn had problems with many people," she said without hesitation. "She was exacting. She could be difficult, sarcastic. A lot of people didn't like her."

"But you liked her."

"Yes. I understood her. She needed things to be a certain way. But I can't think of anyone who disliked her enough to harm her."

"Any business deals that went bad?"

"I'm sure not. Evelyn was good at what she did and scrupulously honest." She stopped, suddenly tearful.

Brisbois gave her a moment, then said, "I get the feeling she and Terri didn't get along that well."

Joan shook her head. "Terri was definitely Carl's girl. But that's not unusual. Mothers and daughters, they do have their battles."

"Battles?"

"Nothing out of the ordinary."

"Clean your room, lose ten pounds, that sort of thing?"

"Yes. Terri isn't like Evelyn. She isn't a perfectionist like her mother. She's softer, more forgiving of people."

Brisbois made some notes. "What do you think Evelyn was doing riding up in the woods?"

Joan shook her head. "Evelyn would never have taken a horse up into the woods. There are no suitable trails up there. Low-hanging branches, animal burrows, tree roots."

"That horse, Ned, did he spook easily?"

"Any horse can be spooked given the right circumstances. But Ned was not particularly skittish, and Evelyn had no trouble controlling him." She hesitated, then said, "I can tell you for certain, Evelyn did not go up into the woods willingly."

Chapter 7

Gregoire stormed up to the desk where Margaret was sorting through the mail. Tim followed. Rudley, who was leaning on the desk, sipping a cup of coffee, tried to pretend he didn't notice them.

Margaret looked up as Gregoire stopped in front of the desk, emitting a long sigh. "What's wrong, Gregoire?"

Rudley put his cup down. "I'm sure what you're going to tell me is going to ruin a perfectly good mood."

Gregoire glanced around, then said in a low voice, "Mrs. Lawrence is driving me insane. First, she has bizarre ideas for the cake. She is thinking of a large bundt with a motorized waterfall at the centre and the figures of the bride and groom posed in the mist at the base."

"If they look as if they're planning to jump, it might be appropriate," said Rudley.

"It is not appropriate," said Gregoire through clenched teeth. "I have planned the most beautiful cake, elegant in its simplicity. The sort of cake you can actually eat. Miss Miller told me to surprise her. She did not say she wanted to be terrorized. This thing Mrs. Lawrence is proposing is outlandish. It is burlesque, the sort of thing you would find in a Legion Hall. The woman is a philistine."

"Don't worry about it, dear," said Margaret. "Tell Mrs. Lawrence you will consider her idea, then go ahead and do what you had planned."

Gregoire was not mollified. "Then she wants flowers in the salad. I have selected a delectable mix of salad ingredients, each one chosen to blend its molecules with a dressing created by me especially for the wedding. I will not have her flowers desecrating my delicate balance."

Margaret thought for a moment. "Why don't you go ahead and prepare the salads you have planned, then to spare Mrs. Lawrence's feelings, do a small piece with the flowers she wants. Mainly for decoration."

"As long as it is inconspicuous," Gregoire said. "I have never felt comfortable working with flowers."

"Perhaps Mrs. Sawchuck will donate a centipede," said Rudley. "That would destroy everyone's appetite for the floral salad."

Gregoire gave him an exasperated look and huffed back to the kitchen.

"Mrs. Lawrence is a pain," said Tim. "She's obsessed with every detail. You would think it was her wedding."

"She wants to be helpful," said Margaret. "I think we should accommodate her, provided Miss Miller is agreeable."

"Mrs. Lawrence is a fanatic," said Tim. He left, shaking his head.

"Flowers in the salad," said Rudley. "I don't know if I could eat a flower, Margaret."

She gave him a playful swat on the arm. "Of course, you could. Your mother told me she couldn't keep you away from her peonies."

"Children will eat anything. Squiggy used to eat mud."

"I think a floral salad would be lovely," said Margaret. "We shouldn't be critical of Mrs. Lawrence. It's fun planning a wedding, considering all the possibilities. We could almost forget…"

"Quite right, Margaret. The wedding is a welcome distraction. Usually we have to devise our own way to muddle through these things." He paused. "I wonder if they've found out who that woman was."

Brisbois and Creighton stood back while the pathologist completed the autopsy. "We have three head injuries," Dr. Jim said. He beckoned them forward. "Here, on the right parietal, we have a superficial lesion overlying a small subdural hematoma."

Brisbois frowned. "Could that have killed her?"

The pathologist nodded. "It could have — eventually — but it didn't." He pointed to the left side of the head. "Here we have a bump."

"A bump?"

"Yes, a simple bump, minor contusion. Probably knocked her out but didn't kill her." He called to the morgue attendant. "Hugh, help me turn her."

The morgue attendant helped the pathologist turn the body to the right.

"The bash on the back of the head killed her," said Brisbois.

"Congratulations," said the pathologist. "Yes, this is what killed our lady. Blunt-force trauma to the occipital area, depressed skull fracture, fragments of bone imbedded in the brain." He left the gurney, threw some x-rays up on the viewer. "She also has a fracture at C-6. Not displaced."

Creighton stared at the x-rays. "How did that happen?"

"From a fall, I would say. She would have survived that, and with appropriate supportive care, would have had minimal residuals."

"The depressed skull fracture," said Brisbois, "what caused that?"

"She was slammed in the head with something heavy."

"What about the one on the right?" Brisbois asked.

The pathologist turned the viewer off. "That was caused by a different instrument, and it probably happened earlier. I can't say how much earlier exactly, but it could have been as much as four or five hours."

"She was hit on the right side of the head first."

The pathologist peered at Brisbois over his glasses. "That's what I just said."

Brisbois returned his stare. "I was thinking out loud."

"The right parietal injury," the pathologist continued, "is a crease, a deep scratch really. It didn't bleed very much. But here's something interesting." He led them to a tray on the counter, picked up a specimen jar. "Here's some stuff I picked out of the wound on the right. Traces of straw, husks, and I think what might be animal manure. This one — the occipital wound — ordinary soil and a partially squashed slug."

"Any ideas about the weapons?"

The pathologist picked up a file folder, opened it, took a glance. "The one on the right? The weapon was thin and fairly heavy. Probably a tool of some kind. The depressed skull fracture? Maybe an irregular piece of sculpture or a rock. Maybe even one of those decorative doorstops. Bring me something. I can probably tell you what it isn't. I might be able to tell you what it is." He put the file aside. "I can tell you all wounds are ante mortem."

"But it was the bash to the back of the head that killed her."

"Yes." The pathologist cast a glance toward the body on the table. "She didn't last long after that."

The doctor stood in front of the door to Carl Hopper's room, arms folded. "I'm afraid Mr. Hopper isn't well enough to see you."

Creighton rolled his eyes. Brisbois cautioned him with an oblique look.

"When do you think he will be well enough?" Brisbois asked.

"Perhaps in a day or two."

Brisbois jammed his hands into his pockets. "What's the problem, doctor? The man fainted."

"The man's wife died. He's depressed and distraught."

Brisbois nodded. "I understand. If my wife had been found dead — possibly murdered — I'd be distraught. I'd also be on the phone, begging the cops to talk to me. I'd want to help the investigation any way I could."

The doctor let his arms fall to his sides. "Mr. Hopper has been sedated. He's sleeping."

Creighton snorted. Brisbois frowned at him.

"OK, doctor," Brisbois said, "when's the soonest we can talk to him?"

"Perhaps tomorrow."

"How about later today?"

"I'll let you know. Please call first."

"How about as soon as he wakes up?" Brisbois smiled. "You wouldn't want to interfere with a police investigation."

The doctor inhaled sharply. "I'll let you know."

Brisbois reached into his pocket, fished out a card. "The minute he wakes up." He grabbed Creighton by the sleeve, urged him down the hallway. They were out in the parking lot before Brisbois spoke. "I'm not sure how much help Mr. Hopper is going to be," he said.

"I'll bet the sedative erased the rest of old Carl's memory cells," Creighton said.

"You don't like the guy very much."

"He's pathetic."

Brisbois patted his pockets for his keys, gave up. Creighton grinned, produced the keys. Brisbois went around the car to the passenger's side. He got in, left the door open, lit a cigarette.

Creighton put the keys into the ignition. "Where to, Boss?"

Brisbois thought for a moment. "The Hopper place. I want to see what our people have turned up."

Simpson stopped as Miss Miller paused beside the brook. He patted Albert on the head, directed him to sit. Albert obeyed. "This looks like a good spot, Elizabeth." He paused. "Or at least as nice as the last several spots we've looked at."

She stood, hands on hips, surveying the site. "I think I like the clearing, although it might be too warm in full sun. We don't want the Benson sisters to faint."

"We could rent a canopy."

"That's a lovely idea, Edward. I don't know if we could have the clearing, though. Detective Brisbois has it cordoned off." She thought for a moment. "Perhaps a spot with dappled light would be better."

He cleared his throat. "I wonder if you've been exposed to Bonnie Lawrence too much."

She looked at him over her glasses. "I'm talking about dappled, Edward. I'm not talking about coordinating the flowers in the salad with the bridesmaids' dresses."

"I thought Mrs. Lawrence's idea of flowers in the salad was a rather nice idea. My mother said that when I was a tot I sometimes refused lunch because I'd eaten so many daisies."

"My mother said I ate Queen Anne's lace." She grabbed his hand. "Come, Edward, let's look a bit more. I'm sure there's a perfect spot over the next hill."

He squeezed her hand. "I'm sure there is."

Brisbois knelt beside the forensics officer. "What have you got, Payette?"

She stood up. "Not much here. The stall's pretty clean. Straw, grain husks, the usual stuff for a stable."

Brisbois levered himself up.

Payette indicated some tools hanging along the wall just inside the door. "We've checked these out. Stevens is looking at the tack room and the tool shed."

"Anything that looks as if it could be the weapon?"

She swept her arm along the display. "Lots of things. There's a shovel here. There's a tool chest in the tack room, hammers, screwdrivers, that sort of thing. There's also one of those carpenter's boxes with the kind of tools a farrier might use for shoeing, trimming hooves, etcetera. Lots of good stuff to commit murder with. We're packaging it up but, so far, nothing looks suspicious."

He digested this. "So maybe she wasn't attacked here."

She wagged a finger. "Don't be so sure about that. Let me show you something." She led him to the doorway, pointed.

He stared at the door jamb. "Blood?"

"Sure is."

He frowned. "Seems kind of low down on the wall. We're thinking she was on a horse."

"Maybe she got on the horse afterwards."

"Doesn't make sense — to get knocked on the head, then get on the horse."

"Maybe she got on the horse to get away," Payette said.

"Maybe." Brisbois stared at the stain. "Definitely not splatter."

"No, it's smear. There're also some smudges on the floor."

"You got specimens?" It was a rumination, not a question.

"We checked the whole stable. This is the only place that registered for blood."

He looked toward the stalls. "Looks as if somebody cleaned out the stalls. Did you check the manure pile?"

She cracked a grin. "We're going to draw straws for that."

He thought for a moment. "Sheffield's at the Pleasant. Who else have we got on the ground?"

"Maroni. He's tracking back from the site."

"OK." Brisbois turned to Creighton. "Let's go see what Maroni turned up."

Miss Miller stepped into a small clearing, stopped. "This looks promising."

Simpson looked around. "It's a pleasant combination of sun and shade. But I'm not sure if it's big enough to accommodate everyone, unless we scatter the guests among the trees. And"—he pointed to a weathered stake—"I'm not sure if it's entirely on the Pleasant's property."

"I think it's Crown land," she said. "But I'm sure the province won't mind." She skipped across the clearing, parted the bushes. "There's another open spot here, Edward."

He followed her, peeked over her shoulder. "Yes," he said, "rather lovely the way the ferns have grown in though the ledges."

Albert tugged at his leash, yipped.

Simpson cupped a hand over Albert's muzzle. "Quiet, Albert."

Albert whimpered, strained toward the ledge.

"He must have seen a chipmunk," Simpson said.

Miss Miller squinted into the foliage. "Look"—she pointed toward the bushes around the ledges—"look at how those branches have been bent over."

He looked in the direction she pointed. "You're right, it doesn't look natural."

She grabbed his hand. "Let's take a closer look." She pulled him after her to the ledge, squealed with delight. "Isn't that clever, Edward? Someone has set up a blind. They've tied cord around those branches and anchored them to that tree." She dropped his hand, started to untie the cord.

"I don't know if you should do that, Elizabeth."

The branches snapped back to reveal an opening.

"It looks like some sort of dwelling," Simpson said.

"Let's take a look."

"I don't think we should."

"I don't think it's occupied. It's probably an abandoned hunting blind." She charged ahead against his protests, swept aside a piece of tattered canvas tarpaulin that covered the entrance. "Edward, look."

He hesitated.

"Edward, come on." Her voice rose with excitement. "Look at this."

Brisbois and Creighton picked their way up the entrance route to the place where Evelyn Hopper's body had been found.

Maroni waved a clipboard as they approached. "We've been trying to get hold of you guys."

Brisbois checked his pocket, grimaced. He had inadvertently turned off his cell phone.

"We've got something for you." The forensics officer turned away, beckoning over his shoulder. "Come on. Keep tight behind me, please."

Maroni led them over an outcropping. A snake slithered over Brisbois' foot.

Brisbois froze. "Jesus."

"What's the matter?"

"Snake."

Creighton peered into the underbrush. "I didn't know you were afraid of snakes."

"I'm not afraid of them. I just don't want them crawling over my feet."

"Here." Maroni stopped, pointed.

Brisbois squinted. "What have you got?"

Maroni hunkered down. "This rock. It was two feet from the body."

Brisbois shoved his hat back. "You think she hit her head on that?"

Maroni smiled. "Could be, but we've got something else for you." He stood, pointed. "Look at that."

Brisbois focused on the low-hanging branch.

"That's hair," Maroni said. "You know what I think happened?"

Brisbois indulged him.

"She catches her hair on that branch. Falls off the horse. Hits her head on that rock."

"Why did the horse run off?" Brisbois wondered. "You'd think he'd stay around."

"He would have if his name was Trigger." Maroni saw Brisbois' face turn into a thundercloud and hastened to add, "Maybe he did for a while. Then he got spooked by a raccoon or something. Horses get weird around little animals."

Brisbois took out his notebook, jotted a few notes. "Anything else?"

"Nothing for now. I'll get some photos. Pack up the rock."

"OK, good work." Brisbois turned away.

Creighton followed.

"It doesn't add up," Brisbois said. "There's a smear of blood on the door jamb. A few spots on the floor. She ends up here, gets clotheslined on that branch, falls off the horse, smacks her head on a rock. The right side of her head barely bleeds, but there's blood on the right side of the door jamb."

Creighton shrugged. "She whacks her head on something in the barn. Her head doesn't bleed, but maybe her nose does. She reaches up to touch her nose, smears the blood on the door. She's kind of wobbly and confused. She can't control the horse. He charges up into the woods. She gets her hair caught, falls off, hits her head on a rock, punches in her skull, breaks her neck. Works for me."

Brisbois stopped, spun on him. "So you're saying it was an accident."

Creighton focused his gaze into the canopy. "Could have been."

Brisbois jammed his hands into his pockets, stamped off. After a few paces, he stopped. Creighton caught up to him.

"There was nothing on her," Brisbois said. "No ID. Nothing." He started off again.

Creighton fell into step. "She decides to give the horse some exercise. Why would she have anything with her? It wasn't as if she was going into town. For all we know, she wasn't planning to leave the property. Like her daughter said, she sometimes just rode around the paddock."

"So where did her stuff go?"

"Maybe she had a little hidey-hole for that stuff. Maybe one of those fake cabbages or something."

Brisbois stopped. "That blood on the door jamb doesn't make sense."

Creighton threw his hands up. "Maybe it wasn't hers."

Brisbois shot him with an index finger. "Right. And?"

Creighton smiled. "Maybe it was her killer's."

"Now you're talking." Brisbois jingled some change in his pocket. "She wasn't wearing her watch. She wasn't wearing her rings. I can see her taking the watch off to ride, but not the rings."

Creighton tipped his hat over his eyes. "So some guy startles Evelyn Hopper in the stable. He whacks her on the head. Her horse gets startled and charges off into the woods. The guy cuts himself somehow. He leaves blood on the door frame. He follows her, finds her lying on the ground. He robs her." He shook his head. "No, I can't really see that. If I were him, if I'd just come into the stable to see what I could grab, I wouldn't confront her. I'd just get the hell out of there."

"Maybe he panicked," Brisbois said. "He followed her to make sure she wasn't going to turn him in. He found her there, lying on the ground, dead. He couldn't pass up the chance to rob her." He stopped, thought for a moment. "Do you think she rode bareback?"

"No."

"Terri said the horse's tack was missing. Does that mean the bridle and the saddle?"

"Yeah, I'd say so."

"So where's the saddle?"

Creighton looked at him, dumbfounded.

"When we saw the horse, all he had on was his bridle."

Creighton shrugged. "Lloyd probably took the saddle off when he hosed him down."

"Let's ask him." Brisbois started off down the hill. "There could be fingerprints."

Creighton chuckled. "I wouldn't count on it. Lloyd probably washed it too."

Margaret hurried up to the desk. "Rudley, I've just heard the most distressing news. That poor woman they found in the woods was Evelyn Hopper."

He stared at her. "Who in hell is Evelyn Hopper?"

"A neighbour on the upper road. She lived on Mr. McGee's old property."

He thought about that. "Well, that makes sense, Margaret. We didn't know who he was either until after he died."

"That was tragic."

He nodded. "A man wearing a tie should never pause to feed a branch into the chipper."

"His son said he was fussy about his property. He couldn't stand to see debris lying about." She sighed. "The point is, Rudley, we should make a greater effort to get to know our neighbours. We shouldn't act as if the lakeshore is all there is to the area."

"On the contrary, Margaret. I think it's perfectly fine. We have enough gruesome deaths to deal with without involving the neighbours."

"Tut-tut, Rudley, we ought to be grateful we have decent people living on the back roads. We could have motorcycle gangs."

"At least they tend to murder their own."

Margaret was about to respond when Brisbois and Creighton entered the lobby.

"Sorry to barge in," said Brisbois, removing his hat. "We were looking for Lloyd."

Rudley leaned over the desk and bellowed, "Lloyd."

Lloyd came down the hallway, hammer in hand.

"That horse you found," said Brisbois. "Did he have a saddle?"

"Nope."

"Saddle blanket?"

"Nope."

Brisbois exhaled slowly. "OK."

"Maybe it fell off," said Lloyd.

"Now, that's rich," said Rudley. "You've got dozens of investigators scouring the woods and you can't find something as big as a saddle."

"Be nice, Rudley."

Brisbois' cell phone rang. "Brisbois." His brows shot up. "OK." He turned to Creighton. "Apparently, Mr. Hopper just woke up."

Carl Hopper lay in bed, the head of the bed elevated to a thirty-degree angle.

"Mr. Hopper," Brisbois began, "I don't know if you remember us — Detectives Brisbois and Creighton."

Carl nodded slightly.

Brisbois helped himself to the vinyl-covered armchair beside the bed. Creighton leaned against the window frame.

"Do you know why we're here, Mr. Hopper?"

Carl blinked. "You're here about Evelyn." He pressed his lips together tightly, then said, "About what happened to Evelyn."

Brisbois nodded. "Yes. We need to ask you a few questions." He paused to make sure he had Carl's attention. "OK?"

"OK."

Brisbois prepared his notebook. "When did you last see your wife alive, Mr. Hopper?"

Carl frowned. "She went riding. That night. The night they said it happened."

"What time?"

Carl hesitated. "I don't know. It was dark."

Brisbois waited, but Carl's gaze has shifted to the window. "OK," he said finally, "take me through this. You saw your wife last night. Did you have supper together?"

Carl moistened his lips. "It was dark. She came in and went upstairs. Then she went out."

"Where did she go?"

Carl looked at him as if he found the question absurd. "She went to the stable."

Brisbois sighed. "You say she came in, then went out. Where did she come in from?"

Carl frowned. "I don't know." He paused, working at a bit of dry skin on his lower lip with his tongue. "Maybe she was just moving her car." He paused, looking deflated. "I don't know."

Brisbois sat back, reviewed his notes. "OK, let's try something else. Tell me about that day. You got up. Where was Mrs. Hopper?"

Carl's gaze drifted to Creighton, then back to Brisbois. "She was in her office at home."

"Go on."

"I had to go into town — Middleton — to the dentist."

"What time?"

"What?"

"What time did you leave the house?"

"Around noon."

"Was Mrs. Hopper still at the house?"

Carl frowned. "In her office."

"Did she say if she had any appointments? Mention she was meeting somebody?"

Carl shook his head.

Brisbois watched him for a moment. "What time did you finish up at the dentist?"

"Around three."

"Then what?"

"I went to the library." Carl hesitated, thought for a moment, "Yes, then I went to the hotel for something to eat. Then I walked home."

Brisbois looked up, surprised. "Why didn't you call your wife to pick you up?"

"I didn't want to bother her."

Brisbois glanced at Creighton. "You know, Mr. Hopper, my wife would have insisted I call her. She would have driven me to the dentist, sat in the waiting room, the whole nine yards."

Carl's eyes showed a glint of life. "She was busy."

"So you walked home."

"I started walking, then somebody gave me a lift."

Brisbois waited, pen poised. "Who was that?"

"I don't know. He said he was staying at the West Wind."

"What time did you get home?"

"I think maybe around five."

"Then what?"

"I fell asleep in my chair."

"Where was Mrs. Hopper at this point?"

Carl shook his head.

Brisbois exhaled slowly. "Was she there when you got home?"

"I don't know. Maybe."

Brisbois tapped his notebook against his knee, three times slowly. "Let's see if I've got this right. You got home from the dentist. You don't know if your wife was there."

"She might have been in her office."

"Wouldn't she have come down to see how you were if she heard you come in?"

"Maybe she didn't hear me."

"Was her car there?"

Carl looked surprised. "I don't know."

"So you fell asleep in your chair. Then sometime after that, Mrs. Hopper came in and went upstairs. Then she came back down and told you she was going riding."

Carl stared at him. "Yes."

"Did you have any other conversation with her — other than that she was going riding?"

"No."

"What time did Mrs. Hopper return from her ride?"

Carl shook his head. "I don't know. I fell asleep on the couch."

"What time did you wake up?"

"Early. It was just before Roslyn got there. Before seven-thirty. She comes then."

"When did you realize your wife was missing?"

"There wasn't any coffee. I thought maybe she'd gone riding."

"You said she went riding the night before."

"Sometimes she does."

"Was there anything that made you think she might not have come home after you fell asleep on the couch?"

Hopper shook his head.

Brisbois flipped back through his notes. "Did anything feel amiss?"

Carl drew a hand across his mouth. "Just the coffee."

Brisbois sat forward, stared at Hopper. "Mr. Hopper, if my wife came home and found me asleep on the couch, she'd wake me up before she went to bed. You know, she'd worry about me getting a stiff neck, sleeping on the couch with one of those decorative pillows. Wives worry about that sort of thing. If she didn't wake me up — if she thought I looked particularly exhausted — and if she had to leave the house before I woke up, she'd leave me a note."

Carl blinked, looked away. "Evelyn wouldn't do that."

Brisbois sighed. "What I'm trying to say, Mr. Hopper, is that if my wife didn't wake me or leave me a note, I'd know something was wrong."

Carl Hopper started to cry.

Brisbois sat at a picnic table in the pocket park enclosed by three wings of the hospital, scratching notes. Creighton ambled up, waving a brown paper bag.

"Two hot dogs all dressed," said Creighton. "Two jelly donuts — raspberry — and coffee. Double sugar for you."

"Thanks." Brisbois opened the coffee, took a sip. "Think he killed her?"

Creighton straddled the bench, unwrapped his hot dog. "I don't think he'd remember if he did. It seems our guy can't handle anything stronger than an Aspirin."

"Some people are like that." Brisbois examined his hot dog. "You didn't put hot peppers on this, did you?"

"Sweet pickle relish."

Brisbois checked his notes. "She worked all the time. They didn't seem to share a social life. She thought he was a wimp. Do you think she had something on the side?"

Creighton bit into his hot dog, chewed thoughtfully before answering. "Don't you think she would have given her best friend just a little hint?"

Brisbois spread a serviette on his lap. "I don't know. She sounds like a pretty cool customer. Definitely not one of your warm and fuzzies. Maybe if she had something on the side, she treated it like business."

"So it doesn't work out," Creighton theorized. "She tries to break it off. He's angry. He comes to her house. They argue. He kills her. Or he calls her. She doesn't want to see him. They argue. She hangs up on him. He comes over, surprises her as she's about to set out on one of her reflective rides. He whacks her."

"Could be," Brisbois said. "But you'd think Carl would have heard something going on."

Creighton sniffed. "Carl was probably sucking his thumb with a pillow pulled over his head."

Brisbois' cell phone rang. He blotted his fingers on the serviette, took the phone from his pocket. "Yeah? What?" His brow creased. "OK, thanks." He jammed the phone back into his pocket, took a bite of hot dog.

"What?" said Creighton.

"That blood," said Brisbois. "Animal blood. Probably equine."

Creighton shrugged. "We know the horse was cut."

"I was hoping it might belong to the murderer." Brisbois uttered a mild oath as the phone rang again.

Chapter 8

Brisbois drew a line across his notebook, wrote: Interview, Elizabeth Miller. "OK, you saw a saddle. Anything else?"

"All sorts of things," said Miss Miller. "Unfortunately," she added, glancing toward Simpson, "I didn't have the opportunity to itemize them."

Simpson cleared his throat. "It didn't seem appropriate to go through someone's belongings."

"We'll have the warrant shortly," Brisbois murmured.

"Detective," Margaret broke in. "The place you're talking about...I'm sure the chap who occupies it had nothing to do with Mrs. Hopper's death."

Brisbois gave her a sympathetic smile. "We don't know anything yet, Margaret."

"He's a hobo," Rudley said.

"He is a vagabond of sorts," Margaret conceded. "He picks up things here and there, but I'm sure he's harmless.

"Brisbois waited, pen poised. "How long has he been camping out up there?"

"We're not sure," said Rudley. "We saw him going through our garbage around Easter."

"We tried to talk to him," Margaret said. "But he was like a stray cat. Finally, Gregoire started putting out food in Tupperware containers. We didn't see him take the food, but, a few days later, the empty containers appeared on the back porch."

"To be washed and refilled," said Rudley.

"I don't suppose he has the facilities to wash dishes," Margaret said. "The point is, he never stole anything from us. Sometimes we left out a few things with the food — socks and so forth. He didn't take anything that wasn't meant for him."

"A scrounger." Brisbois reviewed his notes. "What's this guy's name?"

"Herb," said Rudley.

"We're not sure if that's his real name," said Margaret. "He's known a bit around Middleton. I don't know if he told someone his name was Herb or if someone gave him that name for the sake of having something to call him."

Brisbois closed his notebook, pocketed it. "We'll have a word with him."

Margaret looked distressed. "I'm sure he didn't do anything wrong, Detective. He just picks up things he finds."

"A saddle's a big thing to just pick up."

"Don't frighten him, Detective, or we'll never see him again."

Brisbois' brows shot up. "Would that be such a bad thing?"

She gave him a reproachful look. "It's not cricket to kick a man when he's down."

Brisbois inhaled sharply, nodded, and left. Creighton gave Margaret a wink and followed him out onto the veranda.

"What next, Boss?"

Brisbois fished out a duMaurier, lit it. "What in hell do you think?"

"What's got your goat?"

"A woman hammered to death, that's what."

"I think you're mad because Margaret called you on Herb."

Brisbois turned on Creighton, trailing smoke through his nostrils. He looked defiant, then relaxed. "Margaret's right. We shouldn't go after a guy because he's down on his luck. But that saddle has got to be Ned's. Even if all he did was pinch it, he's got to know something."

Brisbois and Creighton waited on the veranda for the officer to appear with the warrant.

"We could probably get by without one," said Creighton. "According to Miss Miller, the place was nothing more than a cave with a bush for a door."

"Exactly the kind of situation where some judge is going to get pissy." Brisbois hunched his shoulders, looked down toward the dock where Lloyd was helping Bonnie Lawrence into a canoe.

"For someone who says she doesn't care for the country life, she's taken quite a shine to this place," said Creighton.

Brisbois smiled. "I think she likes being fussed over — Lloyd taking her for canoe rides, Tim hovering over her table, all the admiring looks."

"She's a pretty lady."

"I can't say she's my type," said Brisbois.

Creighton gave him a surprised look. "Hey, what's not to like? She's pretty, dresses well, always has a nice smile."

Brisbois watched Lloyd paddle away. "I get the feeling she's always waiting for someone to rescue her. I like a woman with a little spunk."

"Like Miss Miller."

Brisbois lit a cigarette. "I like Miss Miller just fine. I'd like to know if I was up to my ears in quicksand the woman I was with wouldn't just throw up her hands and scream."

Creighton laughed. "Miss Miller would make a rope out of vines or something she learned in Girl Scouts." He gestured toward the departing canoe. "But I don't mind doing a little rescuing now and then."

Brisbois grimaced. "I'm surprised she isn't twirling a parasol."

"She sure isn't like any of the women we've seen here before," Creighton said. "Most of the women here are tough old bats."

"Yeah, otherwise they'd be taking their vacations at some kind of spa."

A cruiser pulled up. Officer Semple alighted and came toward the veranda, holding out the warrant. "Here you are. Signed, sealed, and delivered." He handed the warrant to Brisbois and turned back toward the car.

"Hey"—Brisbois waved the paper at him—"where do you think you're going?"

Semple gave him a blank look.

"You're coming with us."

Semple gave him a wary look. "Where?"

"Up into the woods." Brisbois stuffed the warrant into his breast pocket.

Semple uttered a silent curse.

Creighton chuckled. "Are you worried about getting your shoes dirty? Or are you afraid of falling into a hole, the way you did last time?"

Semple sighed. He waited until they came down from the veranda, then fell in behind them.

Brisbois stopped, checked Miss Miller's map. "This is it." He put up a cautionary hand. "Let's keep cool. If the old guy's in there, we don't want to spook him." He pointed at Semple. "You stay back, over there by the trees, in case he makes a run for it."

Brisbois and Creighton approached the cave.

"Herb?" Brisbois called out.

They waited.

Brisbois signalled to Semple, mouthed, "Be ready." He turned back to the cave. "Herb, it's the police. We'd..."

Before Brisbois and Creighton could react, a dishevelled man erupted from the entrance. He spun off Brisbois, knocking him off balance.

Brisbois took up pursuit. "Get him," he shouted at Semple, who stood rooted to the ground, staring in disbelief.

"Stop. Police," Semple yelled as Herb charged toward him.

Herb lowered his head, driving it into Semple's midsection. A laughing Creighton loped through the trees to find Semple writhing on the ground while Brisbois tried to wrestle Herb into handcuffs.

"A lot of good you were," Brisbois gasped as he finally corralled Herb's left hand.

Semple struggled to his feet .

Brisbois turned to Semple. "You're all right, aren't you?"

Semple uttered a series of squeaks.

"Good boy." Brisbois patted him on the shoulder. "You keep an eye on our friend while we look around. You can do that, can't you?"

Semple finally captured a breath. "I didn't want to pull my gun on him."

"No, no," said Brisbois. "You did the right thing." He turned to Herb, who was struggling against Creighton. "Herb," he said as the old man glared at him, "we've got a warrant to look through your place."

Herb gave Creighton a kick in the shins.

"That hurt," said Creighton. He handed Herb over to Semple.

"I want you to sit down on that stump over there and relax," Brisbois told Herb. "We aren't going to hurt your stuff." He motioned to Creighton.

They ducked in behind the shrubs, swept aside the tarp. Brisbois removed his hat, crouched to enter the cave. He ducked back out, turned to Creighton. "Let's get a team up here. We've hit the mother-lode."

Margaret hovered at the veranda railing as the detectives coaxed Herb into the cruiser. "I can't believe they've arrested Herb. Surely, they don't think he had anything to do with Mrs. Hopper's death."

"I'm sorry," Miss Miller said. She looked chastened.

Margaret turned from the railing. "You couldn't have known." She headed for the lobby. "I must get Rudley. We have to make sure Herb has representation."

Miss Miller returned to the table where Simpson was enjoying an orange squash. "It seemed like such a promising lead," she said.

Simpson nodded. "It did. Of course, the old gentleman may not be a murder suspect. The detectives may have just taken him for questioning."

"In handcuffs?" She paused. "He did have the saddle."

"The man's a scrounge, Elizabeth. The saddle may have slipped off, or he may have found the horse wandering and took what he could." He put the glass down, centring it carefully on the coaster. "Or he may have encountered the victim in the forest and done her in — most savagely, according to what we've heard."

She studied him. "You're developing quite a taste for the macabre, Edward."

He cleared his throat. "I'm afraid the Pleasant does inspire that."

She tented her fingers, stared pensively toward the lake. "You're right. He could have encountered Mrs. Hopper in the forest and bludgeoned her to death. But it doesn't seem likely. According to Officer Owens, Mrs. Hopper wasn't in the habit of riding in the forest at night."

Simpson frowned in concentration. "Perhaps he didn't encounter her in the forest. Perhaps he was in her stable, looking to bed down. He startled her. She rode off into the woods to escape him. He was afraid she might report him to the authorities. He pursued her and murdered her."

"He doesn't look as if he'd have the strength to do that."

He picked up his glass. "People in desperate circumstances often muster unusual strength."

She narrowed her eyes. "According to Tim, Officer Owens suggested that Mrs. Hopper may have sustained the lethal head injury when she fell off her horse and hit her head on a rock. He also hinted she may have received a blow to the head earlier." She paused. "If it weren't for Officer Owens trying to win Tiffany's favour, we'd be completely in the dark. Detective Brisbois has been less than forthcoming."

He gave her a pointed look. "Elizabeth, I don't believe the detective is obliged to share information with us."

She sighed. "You're right, Edward. But he would save himself a great deal of trouble if he confided in us from the start."

Simpson digested this. "Perhaps he realizes we need to focus on the wedding — the bouquets, the favours, the little trifles with our names on them."

She gave him a stern look. "Edward, don't try to distract me."

Aunt Pearl toddled out onto the veranda, took a myopic look around.

Simpson stood, held out a chair. "Aunt Pearl."

She sat down. "Are we talking about the wedding?"

"The murder," said Miss Miller.

"Good." Aunt Pearl leaned across the table. "So what's the latest?"

"Detective Brisbois just took a man away in handcuffs. Herb. I understand he comes around here from time to time."

Aunt Pearl's mouth fell open. "They arrested Herb?"

"They found what they believe to be the victim's saddle among his possessions."

Aunt Pearl sat back. "Herb wouldn't hurt a fly. He's a little rough around the edges, a man of experience. But with a new set of clothes, a haircut, and a shave, you couldn't pick him out of a lineup of Bay Street lawyers."

"A diamond in the rough," said Simpson.

"I didn't know you knew Herb so well," said Miss Miller. "Margaret suggested he kept his distance."

Pearl smirked. "You young people don't always know what's going on. I meet him occasionally. We share a smoke. He's in a state of illiquidity at the moment."

"What do you know about him?"

"He's a travelling man. He goes where the wind takes him. Very romantic."

"Do you know where he's from?"

"Somewhere down the line. For the past few months, he's been staying in the vicinity."

"I understand he lives in that cave in the woods," said Miss Miller.

"He's a rebel at heart." Aunt Pearl sighed. "A James Dean–Jack Kerouac type."

"Obviously, you don't think him capable of murder," said Simpson.

She waved the suggestion off. "Of course not. Herb's the kind of man who lives by his wits." She paused, looked around for Tim. "Besides, he's a gentleman. He would never assault a woman."

Miss Miller considered this. "He came to the Pleasant. Do you think he might have wandered onto Mrs. Hopper's property as well?"

"I don't know. If he had gone there, I imagine he would have got a rude reception. She was that kind of woman. Herb wouldn't have shared that with me. He has his pride."

Miss Miller's eyes brightened. "I didn't know you knew Mrs. Hopper."

"I didn't. But my gentleman friend Nick did."

Miss Miller smiled. "I didn't know you were seeing Nick."

"He takes me cruising every week."

"I thought you didn't like the way he dashed about."

"He's slowed down since his hip surgery." She smirked. "At least as far as the boat is concerned. If you know what I mean."

Simpson blushed.

Miss Miller planted her elbows on the table, resting her chin on her hands. "What does Nick have to say?"

"He says she was pretty snotty, as if she were a few rungs above the rest of us."

Miss Miller's eyes narrowed. "So she may have made some enemies."

"Nick says she treated you according to the size of your boat. He said she was a bit flirty with one man who has a big yacht in port."

"She was married," Simpson said.

Aunt Pearl waved that off. "Since when has that stopped anybody? Besides, Nick says her husband's a wimp."

"Have you told Detective Brisbois any of this?"

"He hasn't asked. Besides, what Nick told me was hearsay, I guess you'd call it. Pillow talk."

Simpson blushed again. "I believe you should tell Detective Brisbois," he said.

Nick Anderson was a small man with thick white hair and a twinkle in his eye that made him look young in spite of his years. "I saw her," he told Brisbois. "She went onto Jim Alva's boat a couple of times."

"Business?"

Nick made a face. "The first time, maybe. His wife was there. The second time..." he shrugged.

Brisbois gave him a nod. "The woman is dead. Nothing you say is going to hurt her."

Nick acquiesced. "She wasn't dressed in a businesslike fashion the second time. The first time, she was wearing something tailored and she was carrying a briefcase. The second time, she was wearing some little sundress and she wasn't carrying a briefcase. They took the boat out and were gone most of the day."

Brisbois made some notes. "What did you think of her?"

"She was a nice-looking woman in a cool sort of way. But she wasn't somebody I'd want to chum around with. Snobbish."

"Yeah?"

"Yeah. I saw her around, off and on. She had a lady friend in town who keeps a boat here. She'd come down with her sometimes. Just the way she treated people, the way she sized things up...the more important she thought you were, the bigger the smile. A lot of people didn't like her."

"I guess she must have made some enemies then."

Anderson pushed back his cap. "Look, Detective, this is a tourist town. A lot of rich people come through here. We're used to people like her. They're just so much grist for the gossip mill. Nobody's going to kill somebody because they act hoity-toity."

"OK." Brisbois thought for a moment. "That second time you saw her getting on Alva's boat, was that the last time you saw her down here?"

Nick shook his head. "No. Last time I saw her, must have been, yeah, it was last Thursday night. I'd just brought my boat in. She drove down to the dock, got out, took a look around, kind of snooty, hands on her hips. Then she got back in her car and burned rubber."

"Burned rubber?"

"Yeah, you know, she ripped out of here, spraying gravel."

"Mad about something?"

Nick shrugged. "I don't know. She always looked kind of pissed off to me."

"Do you remember what time of night that was?"

Nick thought for a minute. "I think it was somewhere around nine. I don't pay that close attention to the time these days." He grinned. "Retired."

Brisbois nodded. "OK." He closed his notebook. "Thanks, Nick. We might need to talk to you later."

Nick gave him a short salute. "Sure thing. I'm always around."

Brisbois and Creighton walked back to the car.

"Thursday night," Brisbois said. "The night she was murdered."

Creighton took out the car keys. "Maybe Alva stood her up," he said.

Chapter 9

The old man's eyes were jaundiced and wild, his skin as creased as a walnut. He sat slumped in his chair in the interrogation room.

Brisbois pushed a cup of coffee toward him. "Relax, we brought you in because we couldn't interview you in the woods." He didn't add "and because I couldn't drag someone who stank like a dead skunk and was as lousy as a badger into Rudley's office" — not that the idea didn't have some appeal. Besides, he wanted the old man to have a shower, some clean clothes, and a decent meal or two. "Look," he said, "we're going to set you up with some new duds, find you a few bucks. Maybe find you a place to stay."

"You can't keep me here."

Creighton recoiled as Herb spewed frothy spit between cracked lips.

"We don't want to keep you here," Brisbois said. "But there is the matter of you assaulting Officer Semple and Detective Creighton and" — he looked at his thumb — "biting me when we were putting you into the cruiser."

"You better not take my place."

"We didn't move your camp," Brisbois said. "We're not Natural Resources."

"Nobody's watching my camp. Somebody'll steal my stuff."

"We brought your stuff in and locked it up." Brisbois folded his arms on the table. "Nobody's going to take it."

Herb gave him a suspicious look.

Brisbois turned to Creighton. "Detective, could you read the list of items we took from Mr. Carey's place?"

Creighton flipped through a sheaf of papers. "One half-package of pipe tobacco — Zig-Zag, and a package of rolling papers. One box of safety matches. A jackknife with a bone handle. Twelve feet of binder twine. Four grocery bags. A shoelace. Two dollars in quarters and four pennies. Two cloth bandanas. A pair of brown canvas sneakers. Three pairs of socks. A pair of long johns. One pair of chino pants. One plaid shirt. One white shirt. One suit jacket. One pair of yarn gloves. One knit toque. One straw hat. One cap with earflaps. One quilted vest. Two fishhooks. Two sinkers. Three bobbers. Thirty feet of nylon fishing line. A package of roofing nails. One pair of boxer shorts. Ten cherry-flavoured lollipops. Six Band-Aids. One booster button for Jean Chrétien. A tin of beans. Four packets of saltines. One TCC subway token." He paused. "One wedding ring. One diamond ring. One ladies' watch. One wallet with forty-five dollars, a debit card, a Visa card, a library card, driver's licence, two grocery receipts, a Lee Valley card, birth certificate, social insurance card. And an OHIP card. All in the name of Evelyn Hopper. And" — he looked at Herb, lifting his eyebrows — "one western saddle and a blue and gold saddle blanket."

Herb glowered.

Brisbois leaned toward him. "I don't think that wallet is yours."

Herb muttered, shuffled his feet.

"Where'd you get it?"

"Found it."

"Where?"

Herb studied the table. "Don't know. Just found it."

Brisbois made a display of smoothing out his notebook, flicking his pen. "OK, you found the wallet. Ever think of giving it back?"

"Was going to. Once I knew whose it was."

Brisbois sighed. "Herb, that wallet belonged to a woman we found dead, not too far from your camp." He turned to Creighton. "What does that paper say about the shirt?"

Creighton shuffled the papers. "It says there was something on the cuff. The lab says it was blood."

"Same type as Mrs. Hopper?" Brisbois asked.

"That's what it says."

Brisbois turned back to Herb. "What do you say to that?"

Fear flashed through Herb's eyes. "You're trying to frame me for something."

Brisbois pushed his notebook away, tilted his chair back. "You saw the wallet lying there. Maybe it fell out of her pocket. You picked it up. Maybe you looked through it to see who she was." He lowered his voice. "You saw the money. Forty-five dollars. That's a lot of money. You were hungry. Running low on tobacco." He paused. "What could it hurt? She was dead."

Herb fished around in his pockets. Came up empty.

Brisbois made a regretful gesture with his hand. "Maybe she wasn't dead, Herb. She fell off her horse. She was lying there, dazed. And you picked up a big rock, so big you could barely get your hands around it, and you smashed her in the head. Then you took her wallet. You took her watch. You yanked off her rings. You took the saddle and blanket off her horse and you walked away. You went up to your place. Maybe you had a bottle. You took a few swigs to celebrate your good fortune. Then you went to sleep and slept like a baby. You didn't know you'd got blood on your shirt."

Herb cogitated on that. "I get blood on my shirt sometimes," he said finally.

"But this was hers."

"Don't know."

Brisbois emitted an exasperated sigh. "Look, the woman's dead. Her blood is on your shirt." He tapped the table to get Herb's attention as he began to follow the progress of a fly across the ceiling. "Herb, I want to help you, but I can't unless you give me some straight answers."

Herb shivered. "I didn't kill that woman. She was gone when I got there."

"Are you sure?"

"I know if something's dead."

Brisbois shuffled through his notebook. "OK, what time did you find her?"

"Late, the moon was moving down."

"Dead?"

"Kind of cold and starchy."

"Did you check her pulse?"

"Don't know that."

"Did you try to wake her up?"

"Nope. She was dead."

"So you took her wallet."

Herb chewed on that. "Didn't figure she'd need it."

"Where was the wallet?"

"Back pocket."

"Kind of like rolling a drunk?"

Herb shot him a hard look. "I'll give you back the wallet. I didn't take anything out of it."

Brisbois sighed. "OK, you took the wallet, then you took the saddle."

"Nope."

Brisbois' eyebrows shot up. "Nope?"

"Took the saddle first."

Brisbois shook his head. "So you found the woman, you took the saddle, then you took her wallet."

"Nope."

Brisbois' shoulders sagged. "Nope?"

Herb gave Brisbois a look that suggested he found him obtuse. "Found the horse down by the creek. Took the saddle and the blanket. Didn't figure he wanted it. Took them back to my place."

"So when did you come across the woman?"

"On my way into town."

"When the moon was moving down."

"Yeah, if I get there early enough, I can get something."

Brisbois made some notes. "OK, while you were going into town, did you see anybody?"

"Seen the guy on the dock. I got some coffee."

"Then what?"

"Just stayed around."

"OK."

Herb fidgeted in his chair. "Can I go now?"

Brisbois shook his head. "No. Even if you didn't do anything to the woman, Herb, there's still the matter of assaulting three police officers."

Herb's face fell.

Brisbois thought for a minute. "Here's what we're going to do. I'm going to talk to my boss. Then we'll get you a lawyer and then we'll figure out what to do next."

"I told you, I don't want one of them. They always get me into trouble."

"We'll see. But I've got to keep you for a while." He paused. "Want something to eat?"

Herb brightened. "Bacon and eggs. Pancakes with real syrup. Coffee."

"We'll have it sent over."

"Maybe a couple of scoops of hash browns, and baked beans, if you have them."

"OK. We'll talk to you again in a bit." Brisbois called to the officer, gave him Herb's order. He walked back to the office, sipping coffee as he went. Creighton followed with a can of 7-Up. Brisbois went to the window, peered out though the blinds, then sat down at the desk. He took out his cigarettes, put the package on the desk in front of him, stared at it.

Creighton perched on the edge of the desk. "What do you think?"

"I don't know."

"Herb says she was in rigor when he found her. Sounds as if he got there sometime between three and four."

"If he's telling the truth."

"If he's telling the truth," Creighton repeated.

"He's got the victim's wallet, her rings and watch, and he's got her blood on his shirt."

"He probably picked up the blood when he took her stuff."

"He could have." Brisbois took out his notebook, flipped through. "He didn't seem to think he'd done anything wrong."

"He needed the money. He figured she didn't. Sort of like taking the boots off a dead soldier. You know what Margaret said — he never stole anything, just scrounged."

Brisbois drained his coffee. "We shouldn't have any trouble keeping him for a while. If we let him go, he'll vanish."

Creighton rubbed his shin. "He could have broken my leg."

"Makes you feel kind of bad, locking him up," said Brisbois. "It's sort of like holding up a bird headed south. He's probably got some kind of survival timetable."

Creighton nodded. "Maybe killing Mrs. Hopper and stealing her wallet was on his survival timetable."

Brisbois thumbed through his notebook. "Yeah, forty-five dollars must have seemed like a gold mine. We'll talk to the Crown."

Chapter 10

Brisbois pushed back his hat, rubbed his forehead. "This case is driving me nuts."

He was sitting on a bench a few yards from the bunkhouse, frowning at his notebook. Creighton sat on the bench opposite, dismantling a maple leaf.

"Tim says there're going to be flowers in the salad at the reception," said Creighton. "Who in hell puts flowers in their salad?"

"My mother," Brisbois muttered. "She grew nasturtiums for her salads."

"You're kidding. My mother used to give me hell for eating the marigolds."

Brisbois nodded. "You can use marigolds. Roses. Day lilies. Almost anything. I like the nasturtiums. They've got that nice peppery bite. Pansies, but mostly because they're pretty. They don't add much for taste."

Creighton made a face. "Don't they have bugs in them? Aphids and the like?"

Brisbois stared at him. "Have you ever seen a tomato worm, or a corn borer? Or a slug?"

"Not that I've known of."

Brisbois gave him an are-you-kidding look.

Creighton shrugged.

"Well, that's the kind of thing you see in your garden from time to time unless you're willing to lace the whole thing with enough pesticide to kill off every songbird within two miles."

"So you're telling me you cook the vegetables up with the bugs."

"No," Brisbois said patiently. "When you pick stuff, you check it for bugs and take them off. There aren't that many. I use organic methods for bug control. That way I don't kill the birds, and the birds help me keep the bug population at acceptable levels. You've seen my garden, haven't you?"

"No."

"Then I've got to get you out for dinner. Mary'd love to have you."

"I'm game."

"OK." Brisbois turned his attention to his notebook. His eyes darted over one page. He flipped ahead, flipped back, brow furrowing. "We've got too many maybes, and everything leads in a different direction." He paused, threw up his hands in exasperation. "Look at this interview with Lloyd." He proceeded to read to Creighton.

Brisbois: *When you got back, what time was that?*

Lloyd: *Just after eleven.*

Brisbois: *And you had Mr. Phipps-Walker and Mr. Lawrence with you.*

Lloyd: *Did.*

Brisbois: *Where'd you let them off?*

Lloyd: *They got off in the parking lot and they walked up.*

Brisbois: *Then what?*

Lloyd: *Went to bed.*

Brisbois: *Did you see anybody moving around?*

Lloyd: *Nope.*

Brisbois: *Was anybody missing?*

Lloyd: *Don't know. Didn't see anybody missing.*

Creighton guffawed.

Brisbois cocked an eyebrow at Creighton, then returned to his notebook. "Anyway, I asked him if any of the cars were missing."

> Lloyd: *Mr. Arnold's car was missing. There were just five cars in the parking lot — Tiffany's, Mr. Lawrence's, Mr. Oliver's, Miss Miller's, and Mr. Carty's.*

Brisbois paused, prompted Creighton with an index finger.

"Carty doesn't have a car." Creighton thought for a moment. "Maybe the car belonged to a visitor or a dinner guest."

"I don't think the dinner guests are here that late." Brisbois pocketed the notebook. "Let's talk to Lloyd."

"Lloyd." Brisbois and Creighton accosted him by the back porch where he was taking a break from gardening.

Lloyd had just settled in with a glass of milk and a piece of pecan pie when the detectives appeared. He liked the policemen but he found it hard to focus on the pie with them around. His mother had taught him it wasn't polite to eat in front of people unless you offered them something.

"Pie?"

Brisbois shook his head. "Oh, no thanks, Lloyd. I just wanted to go over the statement you gave us."

Lloyd grinned. "OK."

Brisbois consulted his notebook. "You said you got into the parking lot just after eleven."

"Did."

"You said there were five cars in the parking lot."

"Yup."

"You said the only car missing was Mr. Arnold's."

"Did."

Brisbois took a deep breath. "Now, when you said somebody's car was in the parking lot, did you mean it was their car or that there was a car parked in that spot that might have belonged to someone else?"

"If I see a car in their place and I see them driving it, it's theirs. But sometimes, like with Miss Miller, the car's in her spot, but Mr. Simpson drives it too."

Brisbois shook his head as if trying to clear his ears. "Right," he said. He returned to his notes. "You said Mr. Carty's car was there."

"Yes'm."

"But Mr. Carty doesn't have a car."

"Was in his spot. Didn't see anybody else driving it so I said it was his."

"The car was in the spot marked for the Oaks."

"Yes'm."

Brisbois frowned. "Don't the cars get registered when the guests arrive?"

"Do."

"What if one of the other guests had a visitor or there was a guest in for dinner, might they park in one of the other guests' spots if that guest didn't have a car?"

"Could."

"Would they let somebody know if they had done that?"

"Would if they was nice."

"But, if no one complained, a dinner guest could park in Mr. Carty's space and no one would know."

"Could, but most of them aren't here so late."

"But somebody visiting one of the other guests might be."

"Guess so."

Brisbois thought for a moment. "Do you remember what the car in Mr. Carty's space looked like?"

"Yes'm."

Brisbois prompted him with a hand gesture.

"Kind of old. Purple like lilacs. Honda Civic."

"Ontario plates?"

"Yes'm."

"Anything special about it? Broken taillight, that sort of thing?"

"A couple of dings. And it was a college car."

"A college car?"

"Said in the back window. Carleton University."

Brisbois turned to Creighton. "Well, I'll be damned."

"Knew it wasn't a dinner guest," said Lloyd, "because it was there two nights."

Brisbois meandered down the lawn in the general direction of the dock, digesting the interview with Lloyd. "That car in Carty's parking space sounds a hell of a lot like Terri Hopper's."

Creighton put a hand on his hat as the brim lifted in the breeze. "So she lied to us."

"Sounds like it." Brisbois skidded to a stop. "What do you suppose she was doing here?"

"Maybe her being here explains what a young guy like Carty was doing here. Terri's his girlfriend. She was staying with him. She tells her parents a little white lie. Then her mother gets murdered, and the lie doesn't seem so little anymore."

"But why wouldn't she take him home?"

"Things weren't so great at home. Why would she want to drag him into that?"

Brisbois stared at the ground for a moment. "Maybe." He didn't sound convinced. "We know she didn't have a great relationship with her mother. Maybe she did take him home. Her mother didn't approve. Things got out of hand."

"You're saying Terri killed her mother?"

"Maybe. Or maybe she had help."

"Or," said Creighton, "maybe Evelyn lights into Terri. Terri storms out. Carl's upset about the way Evelyn treated Terri. They have a fight about it. He kills her. Aunt Joan said she was Carl's girl."

"That's not a bad theory." Brisbois' cell phone rang. He dug it out of his pocket. "Yeah." He listened, nodded. "OK." He pocketed the phone and headed toward the car. "Come on. Doc wants to talk to us."

The pathologist motioned toward the tools laid out on the table. "I've examined the stuff your people collected and I think I've found some likely culprits." He hauled out a heavy, narrow shovel with a flat, sharp end. "The cut on the right parietal and the one on the horse's shoulder? They were caused by something like this. But not this particular item."

Brisbois' brow crinkled.

"This one's clean."

"Clean?"

"Garden soil. That's what's on this one. No straw, no manure, no husks, no blood. But something exactly like this did it. Just not this one."

"So there were two similar shovels in the stable. Someone whacked Mrs. Hopper and the horse with one and took it with him."

The pathologist regarded him over his glasses. "You're the detective. But let me show you how I think it could have happened."

Brisbois gave him a go-ahead gesture.

The pathologist picked up the shovel, stepped aside, raised it over his head. "Now, if your victim was mounted, and you're swinging upward, you're not generating a lot of force at this angle."

"So she was just grazed."

"Right, but on the downswing, you get a little more punch. You've got gravity to help for one thing. That's why the horse got the worst of it."

"But the shovel didn't kill her. You told us that before. The blow to the right side of her head wasn't fatal."

The pathologist laid the shovel on the table. "No. It struck her hard enough to give her a small subdural, which, as I said, might have killed her eventually — maybe days later." He shrugged. "Maybe never." He reached into a cardboard box that sat on the table near the shovel, took out a large rock. "Now this is more interesting."

Brisbois and Creighton stared at the rock.

The pathologist placed the rock upside down on a metal tray, pointed to the gritty surface. "This is the surface that made contact with her skull. She didn't fall and hit her head."

"Somebody picked the rock up and bashed her with it."

"Yup, and let me show you something." The pathologist picked up a manila envelope, took out some photographs. "See?" He pointed to the upper part of the photograph. "The rock was moved. Somebody picked it up, bashed our lady's skull in, then put it back down. That person didn't get it exactly in the right position, but I think he tried."

Creighton studied the pictures. "Couldn't somebody just have kicked the rock, moved it by accident?"

The pathologist shook his head. "No, that would have left gouge marks in the soil, I think. We don't see that. And there should have been a little lip where the soil was pushed aside. And," he said in conclusion, "this side of the rock was sitting on top of the grass around it. It overlapped by a centimetre." He nodded emphatically. "That rock was picked up and put back down."

Brisbois thought for a moment. "Any chance the forensics team moved it?"

"No. Maroni was very careful. He photographed it, then brought it in in situ. He cut out thirty centimetres square of the forest floor. The lab's playing with that now."

"Any fingerprints on that?"

"No. The upper surface is too irregular. The lab noted some marks in the muck on the bottom suggestive of fingerprints." The pathologist pointed them out to Brisbois and Creighton. "As you can see, they're too smudged to say for sure."

"Trace?"

"Maroni noted some fibres in his report. Off-white. They've gone to Trace, but the opinion is cotton."

Brisbois walked out of the office and halfway down the hall before stopping. "Off-white cotton," he said to Creighton. "Could be from a million places." He fondled his cigarette package. "Herb was wearing a red plaid shirt, an old yellow vinyl raincoat." He shook his head. "It's got to be eighty degrees, and the guy's wearing long sleeves and a rubber coat."

"These guys are all the same," Creighton said. "They're afraid to lose their coats. They're afraid if they take them off, somebody will steal them. Some of them are afraid of catching cold, but more often they're hiding needle tracks or protecting themselves from alien death rays and CSIS wiretaps."

"They might be right about that one."

Chapter 11

Several of the guests had gathered around the wicker tables on the veranda. Tim brought a tray of sandwiches and iced tea and placed them on the sideboard. Aunt Pearl selected a salmon sandwich and a glass of tea. She returned to the table she was sharing with Miss Miller, Mr.Simpson, the Lawrences, and Mr. Bole. Jack Arnold sat alone on the settee adjacent. Aunt Pearl rummaged in her purse and came up with a flask. She emptied half of the contents into her glass.

Detective Brisbois and Detective Creighton had conducted another round of interviews that morning.

"I don't know what more the detectives expect me to tell them," Aunt Pearl said. "I didn't see or hear anything. I sleep like a log. There could have been a Salvation Army band playing 'Onward Christian Soldiers' under my window and I wouldn't have known."

"They wanted to know if I had noticed anything while returning to my cottage," Mr. Bole chipped in. "I don't recall anything unusual." He shrugged. "After all of my years coming to the Pleasant, I'm sure I would have noticed if something was afoot."

Tee Lawrence reached for his drink. "There wasn't a soul around when we returned from our fishing trip."

"I went straight to my cabin," Bonnie said. "Right after dinner. I didn't go out again until breakfast the next morning." She sighed. "I don't know what the detectives thought I could have seen."

"Would you care for something?" Mr. Bole asked Arnold as he caught him staring at their table.

"No." Arnold got up and went to the sideboard.

"I think I caught Mr. Arnold ogling the ladies," said Mr. Bole. "That's a habit of his I find offensive."

"I believe he's simply gauche," said Simpson. "We should have asked him to join our table."

Mr. Bole gave him a dubious look. "I must say you're a generous soul, Simpson. I expect, at one time, they might have called you a good Christian. I'm afraid the truth is Mr. Arnold is a Neanderthal who chooses to flout conventional good manners."

"Edward would give the Devil the benefit of the doubt," said Miss Miller. "He would say he was an abused child with a fire fetish." She gave Simpson a fond look. "It's an admirable quality I'm afraid I don't share."

"Me neither," said Mr. Bole. "But I agree it's a trait worthy of emulation."

Jack Arnold filled his plate with sandwiches and turned. He paused as he passed the table, fixed Bonnie Lawrence with a mocking stare. She coloured and turned away.

"We've got the Reverend Pendergast," Margaret said. She made a note on her program. "I'm sure he'll do well. I doubt if he's forgotten how to perform a wedding ceremony in spite of his memory deficits. I'm sure it's just one of those age-related problems where the most recent things are what's forgotten."

"In that case, we should send someone to get him the morning of the wedding. Our biggest concern may be that he's forgotten there *is* a wedding." Rudley shook his head. "Margaret, I hope that damned detective has his problems wound up before the day. The last thing we need is him here, pestering the wedding guests. It's bad enough that he's been plaguing everyone all morning."

"Rudley, it seems to be a difficult case. I'm sure he's getting frustrated."

"And I'm getting frustrated with him."

She patted his arm. "Buck up. I think he's away at the moment."

"Yes, he is," said Rudley. "He's trying to find young Carty to harass him. I made the mistake of telling him he had taken a canoe out."

Brisbois scanned the lake with binoculars as the car inched along the shore road. "Bingo," he said. "Pull over here."

"That's him?"

"Yup." Brisbois lowered the binoculars. "Caught him red-handed. I'm looking forward to hearing his explanation for this."

Creighton followed the path of a canoe that was making its way toward shore. "Are we going to hide in the bushes and spy on him or just watch him from here with the binoculars?"

Brisbois got out of the car, closed the door, and lit a cigarette. "We'll wait until they come ashore with their picnic lunch, then we'll go down. Maybe they'll invite us for a bite."

They watched as Rico hopped out of the canoe in shallow water. He reached back and grabbed the picnic basket. Terri Hopper jumped into the knee-deep water and pulled the canoe onto the shore.

"Looks as if he had Gregoire make him up a lunch," said Creighton.

Brisbois trained his binoculars on the basket. "It's not one of Gregoire's. He always puts a checkered cloth over the top."

Terri took out two packages and unwrapped them.

"Sandwiches in plastic wrap," said Brisbois. "Now we know for sure it's not one of Gregoire's. He uses waxed paper." He paused, put the binoculars away. "I think it's time to go. She just gave him a big kiss."

"Seems a shame to disturb them."

Brisbois grabbed a branch as he eased down the embankment. "Better now than later."

They reached the cove, paused behind a sweep of weeping willows. They could hear Terri giggling.

Creighton peeked through the branches. "She's feeding him potato chips," he whispered.

Brisbois shook his head. He parted the bushes and stepped out. "Mr. Carty, Miss Hopper."

They turned. Terri stared, slack-jawed. Rico tugged at a chip that had stuck to his lower lip. Creighton hooted.

"I came down with Rico," Terri said. Her gaze was focused on Rico, who stood a few yards away, talking to Detective Creighton. "I stayed with him the first two nights. We didn't tell anybody because we couldn't afford to pay for both of us."

"What did you do?" Brisbois asked. "Just hide out in the cabin?"

She looked at him, downcast. "The first day. The next day, I left really early, around five."

"Where did you go?"

"I went into Middleton. I got something to eat. Then I slept in my car until it was time to show up at home." She took a deep breath. "Then everything happened." She bit her lip to stifle a sob.

He waited her out.

"Us staying together in Rico's room, that's the only thing we didn't tell you the truth about," she said.

He gave her a moment to collect herself, aware of Rico watching them anxiously. "OK, Terri, that night, the night your mother was murdered, where were you?"

She caught her breath. "I was with Rico. We had dinner."

"Where did you have dinner?"

"In Rico's cabin. Rico ate in the dining room. He asked for a doggy bag. For me. Rico took the dishes back up to the kitchen around nine. He was afraid if he didn't, someone might come to get them. We watched the baseball game." She hesitated. "Then we went to sleep."

Brisbois kept her waiting while he wrote some notes. "Your parents have a big house, Terri," he said, looking up at her. "Why didn't you take Rico home?"

Terri wiped a hand across her eyes. "I had to tell Mom first. I had to tell her Rico and I were engaged."

Brisbois smiled. "Congratulations. He seems like a nice young man."

"He is." Her voice took on an edge. "Mom had met Rico before and she wasn't very nice to him. I wanted to make sure…"

"That she didn't create a scene," Brisbois finished.

Terri nodded.

"What did your mother have against Rico?"

She hesitated. "She didn't think he was right for me."

Brisbois glanced toward Rico. "Was it because he wasn't tall enough or blond enough?"

Terri bent her head. "Mom could be real snotty about some things."

He paused. "Look, Terri, here's the way I see it. You're going to see your mother to tell her you're going to marry somebody she doesn't approve of — because he's too short and too dark. She gets nasty, says hurtful things about someone you care about. Maybe things got out of hand."

She shook her head vigorously. "No, it didn't happen like that. I would never do anything like that."

"Maybe not by yourself."

She stared at him. "Rico wouldn't hurt anybody. He knew what my mother thought. He was OK with it. He's a very secure guy. He doesn't have problems with self-esteem. He thought my mother would come around — eventually."

"And you?"

"I thought she would have too. Mom could be snotty, but if she'd had a chance to see Rico with the horses, I think she would have come around. They both love horses."

He changed course. "How long have you known Mr. Carty?"

"Almost three years."

"You said your mother had met him."

"We had dinner a couple of times when Mom was in Ottawa on business."

"So she knew he had been in the picture a while."

"Yes, but I think she thought it wouldn't last. We didn't make an issue of it. That we were together. But when we got engaged, we wanted to tell her and Dad together."

"So you rented a cabin here in case she didn't take to the idea."

"Yes. It was the closest, and if Mom made a fuss, I could still see Rico." She paused. "I'm sorry about not telling the innkeeper. I'll get a cheque from work in a couple of days. I'll pay the extra." She looked at Brisbois in desperation. "That would make it all right, wouldn't it?"

"If she killed her mother, she put on a pretty good act," said Brisbois. "She seems to think our main gripe is they didn't pay Rudley for double-occupancy."

Brisbois and Creighton sat in the Crown's office, reviewing the case.

"So you're prepared to eliminate Miss Hopper and Mr. Carty as suspects?" The Crown looked up from his papers, his expression hopeful.

"For the most part, her story sounds sincere," said Brisbois. "I don't think she and Mr. Carty killed Mrs. Hopper, but I think she's holding something back."

The Crown ran his pen down the list, settled on Carl Hopper's name. "Do you think she's protecting her father?"

"Could be."

"OK," said the Crown, "make the case for Carl Hopper."

Brisbois flipped through his notes. "He certainly had opportunity. Motive? Well, it sounds as if the marriage was falling apart. Maybe the wife was having a fling. Maybe that ticked him off. But maybe it was more about money than love. The guy's got the life he wants. He's a writer. He's got a great place to work. By all accounts, he loves being a gentleman farmer. If the marriage is in trouble, if the wife wants a divorce, he could lose all that."

"Pretty good motive."

"Yeah."

"Any physical evidence?"

"Nothing conclusive. He had straw and manure in the crevices of his shoes. Big deal. He lives on a farm."

"What about his clothes?"

"The housekeeper says his clothes were pretty dirty but she didn't notice any blood," Brisbois said. "He told her he'd had a fall."

"I understand there wasn't much blood on the premises."

"No. Just the few smudges mentioned in the report."

"No lab on the clothes?"

Brisbois shook his head. "First, the housekeeper couldn't remember what he was wearing. To top it off, she'd done the laundry."

The Crown frowned. "Is that one of her usual duties?"

Brisbois nodded. "She's there three days a week. She does the cleaning, the laundry, makes meals."

Creighton grinned. "She does everything for Carl but wipe his ass."

"He's kind of inept," Brisbois said.

"So you have nothing conclusive on his clothes and you can't tie him to a murder weapon."

Brisbois exhaled forcefully. "No. The shovel they took from the stable, the one the coroner says…"

"I read the report." The Crown shrugged. "Is there a shovel missing?"

"We don't know for sure. Carl's fuzzy about that. The daughter says she can't remember. The housekeeper has no idea."

"So we don't know."

"No."

"Anything else?"

"We checked out Carl's account of his activities in town that day. The hotelier said he was pretty woozy when he left the dining room. The dental receptionist said he seemed pretty shaken by the procedure — more than most patients, she said."

"I thought he just had a tooth pulled."

"It was a big molar," Brisbois said. "Apparently, it broke off and the dentist had to do a lot of digging around."

The Crown put a hand to his cheek. "Ouch."

"The guest at the West Wind" — Brisbois paused to check his notes — "Bill Czigler. He confirms he picked Carl up about a mile out of town that day. Said he came across him weaving along the road. Said he thought he was drunk, but since he didn't look dangerous, he offered him a ride. He left him at the laneway to his place. After that, we have only Carl's word for what went on."

"As a suspect, he's a keeper, but we don't have enough to charge him with anything."

"Not yet."

The Crown continued down his list. "Then you have the vagrant. Mr. Herb Carey. He had the victim's blood on him and he had some of her possessions." He flipped a page. "The shrink says he's a flight, not a fight guy."

"The housekeeper says Mrs. Hopper ran a tramp off the property a few months ago. He was bedding down in an empty stall. He didn't offer any resistance. He grabbed his stuff and ran. After that, he became a regular visitor at the Pleasant. They think he was sleeping in the attic of the coach house when it was colder. They didn't disturb him. Now he's living in a cave in the woods."

"He got aggressive with you."

"We were preventing his flight. We don't want to make a big deal about the assaults but we would like to keep him around."

The Crown turned a page. "The shrinks have him signed in for seventy-two hours. I'm guessing they won't be able to keep him past that. Brian Allin has already been around to discuss the charges — the theft and so forth."

"Brian Allin?"

"Yes. I understand the Rudleys are picking up the tab."

Brisbois smiled. "Margaret Rudley is a generous lady."

"Has all of Mrs. Hopper's property been recovered?"

"Minus what Herb spent on breakfast."

"Essentially recovered." The Crown dropped his pen. "I'm not interested in prosecuting the old sod for five bucks."

"He was at the scene. He had the victim's blood on him."

The Crown gave Brisbois a long look. "Allin is already making noises about the evidence being circumstantial." He flipped through the pages. "We know he was in the woods. He lives there. He crossed Mrs. Hopper's path because he was on his way into town to see what he could scrounge at the dock. He did that every morning. We know he took her stuff, but do we have any evidence he was at her place that night?"

Brisbois shook his head. "We can't tie him to the stable. His running shoes were clogged with mud and grass but no straw or oats. We don't have the complete trace yet."

"Apparently, Margaret Rudley has offered to act as his surety. Does this lady go out of her way to cause herself trouble?"

"Kind-hearted lady. Good for handouts," said Brisbois. "Hobos' language," he added, catching the Crown's quizzical look.

"We'll keep him as a suspect," said the Crown. He checked his list. "Moving on, we have Mr. Jack Arnold. He had an unfortunate encounter with the lady in the hotel bar that night. He ended up abandoning his car and, apparently, wading through a swamp. But it doesn't look as if you have anything to link him to the crime scene."

"Nope, and the bartender confirms what Arnold told us. Mrs. Hopper was in the bar before Arnold arrived. The bartender got the impression she was waiting for someone, but not Arnold."

The Crown shook his head. "It's Grand Central Station up there. You've got Mrs. Hopper's horse running around, Mr. Arnold mucking around in the swamp, the waiter and the cook trotting trays around, the local hobo. And you've got Mr. and Mrs. Rudley camped out in the middle of all that. Did you ever think they might have done it?"

"Are you serious?"

"Not really, but you'd think they would have heard something."

"The Rudleys heard a lot of snap, crackle, and pop throughout the night. They thought it was just the usual animal suspects."

"OK." The Crown studied his notes. "What about this James Alva?"

Brisbois shrugged. "It would seem that he and Mrs. Hopper were having a little tryst. But the night of the murder, he was home with his wife."

"Can anyone but his wife corroborate that?"

"Creighton and I interviewed the neighbours." Brisbois checked his notes. "One of them, Miss Lily Casselman, saw him come home around seven p.m. She's sure he didn't leave the house after that."

"She keeps that close an eye on him?"

"Apparently, her dog makes a fuss whenever he starts his car up," Brisbois said. "Tony Verbeek, the neighbour whose property abuts Alva's at the back, says he saw Mr. Alva on his patio around ten-thirty."

The Crown took off his glasses, polished them, and set them aside. "Is there anyone else you'd like to consider?"

"Mrs. Hopper might have been having an affair with any number of people," Brisbois said. "We're working our way through her appointment book."

"And of course there are the several thousand people in the vicinity," Creighton murmured.

The Crown threw him a sharp look.

Brisbois shrugged. "Mrs. Hopper was not a well-liked woman."

Chapter 12

"Detective." Miss Miller accosted Brisbois and Creighton as they came up the walk.

Brisbois tipped his hat. "Miss Miller."

"I hear you strongly suspect that Carl Hopper killed his wife."

He smiled. "I strongly suspect a lot of people."

"I have given the matter some thought," she continued, ignoring his remark. "And I think you're on a wild-goose chase."

Brisbois stopped, sank down onto a bench, invited her to join him. "We'd hate to break our perfect record."

She gave him a look that said she would let that bit of sarcasm pass. "I've been studying his novels."

"I've heard he's pretty good."

"He isn't F. Scott Fitzgerald, but he's not bad. However, that's not what's relevant." She set her chin. "After perusing several of his books, I'm convinced he couldn't have murdered his wife."

"I'm glad I haven't read any of his books."

She gave him an exasperated look.

He offered an apologetic shrug.

"His writing shows considerable respect for women, particularly strong women. In confrontation with such women, even strong evil women, his male protagonists always engage them in a respectful manner. Those who choose not to confront their female adversaries either withdraw to discernment or self-destruction."

Creighton shrugged. "Who's to say he identifies with these wimps?"

Brisbois winced. Miss Miller fixed Creighton with a steely stare.

"I believe writers create from their own sensibilities, Detective," Miss Miller said, "and Carl Hopper does not advocate violence against women."

"That's an unusual defence, Miss Miller," Brisbois said. "Not guilty by reason of library."

She punished him with a few moments of stony silence, then said, "From what I've been able to glean, Carl Hopper has no history of violence. He doesn't even lose his temper."

Brisbois smiled. "As always, Miss Miller, we will take your theories under advisement."

She gave him a disparaging look. "No, you won't." She smiled, got up, and marched away.

Brisbois looked after Miss Miller. "What do you think about that, Creighton?"

Creighton shrugged. "I don't think you can tell what somebody's like by reading their books."

Brisbois massaged his neck. "She's partly right. Carl Hopper is passive. He's never shown any signs of aggression."

Creighton kicked at a pebble. "I don't know if that means anything. We've seen guys do slow burns for years, then finally erupt in a big way. And everybody is astonished. He was such a nice, quiet guy, they say. Just because the guys in his novels are five-star feminists doesn't mean he doesn't have a capacity for violence if the situation's right."

Brisbois gave him a surprised look. "Hey, I like your theory better than Miss Miller's."

"Thanks, Boss." He jingled some change in his pocket. "I hear they're having a card tournament tonight. What happened to Music Hall?"

"I hear they're holding it the Friday after the wedding."

"Too bad. I was looking forward to it."

Brisbois gave him a poke in the arm. "You could still go. Get a date. Bring her for dinner and the show?"

Creighton considered this. "I don't think it would be the same coming here if there wasn't a murder going on."

Brisbois shrugged. "Maybe you'll get lucky."

Mr. Bole examined his hand. "I would say this is a lay down."

Norman gave him an irritated look. "I think we should play it out."

"As you wish, Norman. But I warn you, you're snookered."

Tim paused at their table to check the refreshments. "Would you care for anything?"

"I'll have some pretzels with that lovely mustard dip," said Geraldine.

"I think you should concentrate on your hand, Geraldine," said Norman.

"Norman's very competitive," Geraldine whispered to Tim. "The pretzels and dip would be nice."

"I'll have a glass of white wine," Bonnie said.

"Coming right up." Tim walked away, chuckling. He went into the kitchen, filled a bowl with pretzels. "Mrs. P-W loves your mustard dip," he told Gregoire.

"Of course she does," said Gregoire. "It is my own invention."

"Norman doesn't have any better luck at bridge than he does at fishing," said Tim. He added a glass of white wine, a bowl of rice crisps, and a plate of cheese to his tray and returned to the ballroom. He deposited the pretzels and dip with Geraldine as Norman grimly played out his losing hand.

"If you're going to be a grouch, Norman, I'll play the next hand with Mr. Bole," Geraldine said. "Although, in your current state, I'd hate to inflict you on Mrs. Lawrence."

"Oh, I'm sure Mr. Phipps-Walker wouldn't be an imposition," said Bonnie.

"And I won't have a conniption if you get mustard dip on the cards," Mr. Bole told Geraldine.

Tim hurried back into the kitchen. "Better make up a rum and Coke for Norman," he told Gregoire, "he's about to blow a gasket."

"One rum and Coke coming up," said Gregoire.

Tim took the drink and returned to the ballroom, where Geraldine had traded places with Bonnie Lawrence.

"Five clubs," said Norman.

Mr. Bole studied his cards. "Pass."

Bonnie stared at her cards, then said. "Pass."

"Pass," said Geraldine as Norman spluttered.

"I was responding to your 4NT bid," Norman howled. "I didn't intend to be left in five clubs."

"I'm sorry," Bonnie whispered. "I don't know where my mind was."

"I guess this is going to be a lay down too," Mr. Bole chuckled.

Norman grabbed his drink and took a healthy slug.

"I'm sorry." Bonnie stood up. "I think I'll go watch the euchre tournament. If you can find someone to sit in…"

"There's Miss Dutton," said Mr. Bole. "She's always good for a hand." He waved to Pearl, who was wandering toward them with a drink in her hand.

Bonnie gave Norman a nervous pat on the shoulder and left.

"I thought she was supposed to be a decent club player," Norman fumed. "I thought even an occasional player would know the classic Blackwood's convention."

"Perhaps she's accustomed to a different terminology," said Mr. Bole, giving Geraldine a conspiratorial wink.

"All I know," said Norman, "is she managed to put us into a contract we didn't have a hope of making."

Mr. Bole chuckled. "You're right, Norman. You didn't."

Norman turned to Aunt Pearl, who was awaiting the deal. "Do you know Blackwood's convention, Miss Dutton?"

She smirked. "I'll have you know, I was a county champion in my younger years."

"I didn't know that," said Mr. Bole.

"I don't like to brag."

Norman gave Mr. Bole a Cheshire-Cat smile.

Jack Arnold left the inn at nine-thirty. He stopped to check his watch, then wandered out onto the dock and turned to look back at the inn. The lights winked as the leaves wobbled in a light breeze. He cursed, swatted at his neck as a mosquito sunk its proboscis into his sunburnt flesh.

"You'd think the booze would keep them away," his wife used to say.

She'd made a lot of remarks like that the last few years of their marriage. Said he reeked of booze, used it as an excuse to banish him from their bedroom and, finally, from her life.

He waved off another attack, lit a cigarette. He missed his wife when he remembered the early days, when he remembered her as his partner, the woman who kept the books, helped load the truck, answered the phones, did damn near everything back then when he had nothing but a truck and the know-how to build houses. Hell, back then, he was doing menial repair work half the time. She had two babies to look after, and still did everything she could for him.

Then he got successful. She stopped keeping the books. He acquired an office staff. She devoted most of her time to the kids. He couldn't say he missed the kids; he barely knew them. Building a business had been a rush; keeping it going proved stressful. He'd always been a pretty good drinker. He got better. Women followed. There was a certain type of woman who thought he was something because he owned a fleet of trucks with his name on them. Groupies. He didn't miss that. Then there were the women whose husbands were running around on them. They needed a shoulder to cry on, and he was happy to offer his. The fact that he was running around on *his* wife didn't seem to bother them. Maybe they thought his infidelity was more righteous.

He took a long drag on his cigarette, coughed. The woman who was so eager to help him build his business proved just as enthusiastic about taking it away from him. By the time she was finished, he was in debt up to his ears.

He knew he shouldn't have booked a fishing trip this year — he really couldn't afford it. But he needed it. He had chosen the Pleasant because he'd heard the fishing was good and because he'd worn out his welcome at every other place he could think of. Something about offending the women guests. He sniffed. Women were brainwashed these days, looking for excuses to take offence.

He flicked an ash from his cigarette, winced as the breeze blew an ember against his cheek. He was feeling a little logy. Maybe tomorrow he'd take out a boat, do a little fishing, laze around on the veranda in the afternoon, enjoy the cooking. When he got home, maybe he'd cut down on the booze, start going to the gym. Once he got cleaned up, got his business back on sound footing, he might meet a nice woman, maybe somebody as good as his wife. He paused. Almost as good.

He flicked his cigarette into the lake. Tonight, for the first time in a long time, he could see the light at the end of the tunnel.

Chapter 13

"Only a few more days to go, Rudley," said Norman as he stopped at the desk. "How are you holding up?"

Rudley allowed himself a smug smile. "Quite well, Norman. I'm happy to say everything is under control."

"You must be enjoying the novelty of that." Norman paused as Rudley glowered. "What I'm saying is, that as organized as you and Mrs. Rudley are, external forces seem to conspire against you."

Rudley signed off an invoice with a flourish. "Not this time."

"Then preparations are going well?"

"Perfectly. We have box upon box of paper rosettes made from thrice-recycled paper, destined after the nuptials to join Lloyd's worm farm, dozens of heart-shaped cookies to be placed under pillows."

"In lieu of slivers of wedding cake?"

"Miss Miller and Mr. Simpson have requested a cake the guests can actually eat. Good idea. I've always found those three-tiered fruit cakes a waste."

"Geraldine and I had a three-tiered cake made entirely of suet and birdseed — so our feathered friends could share our special day."

"I think I'll pass on that, Norman. I don't want the gulls bombarding us with their thanks."

Norman looked confused, then brightened. "Oh, there's Geraldine. Better hurry or we won't get our spot."

There's a panoramic view from every seat in the dining room, Rudley thought, and he wants the one that gives him a view of his fishing hole. He's probably hoping he'll figure out why everyone except him manages to haul something out of it.

Margaret came into the lobby, trailing a streamer composed of tiny Union Jacks. "What do you think, Rudley?"

"Rule Britannia."

"I thought I'd drape these over the veranda railing to make Edward's parents feel welcome."

"We could dress Lloyd up as a Beefeater and stick him in a flowerpot."

She gave him an aggrieved look. "I believe you're being sarcastic, Rudley."

"I apologize, Margaret, but I thought the idea was to keep the ceremony simple. The happy couple indicated all they wanted was a simple ceremony, a nice meal with friends, and our good wishes."

She gave him a swat on the arm. "I know they said that and I have no doubt they are sincere. The fuss is for the parents. And the guests. Everyone is so excited. Everyone wants to contribute. The Benson sisters are making up those little cones for sweetmeats, the Sawchucks will be taking candid shots for a special album, Mr. Bole has worked his fingers to the bone, putting together a wedding medley. Gregoire has created several original dishes. He's outdone himself again and again. Our young couple has nothing to do but show up." She beamed. "And I'm so looking forward to seeing you in your tuxedo. It's been far too long."

"Not nearly long enough," he murmured.

"You'll look dashing for the photographs."

They looked up as the lobby door opened. Tiffany came in, walked straight to the desk without a word, and stopped, her forehead puckered.

Margaret and Rudley exchanged glances.

"Is there anything the matter, Tiffany?" Margaret ventured.

"Mr. Arnold is asleep," she said.

Margaret glanced at the clock. "He's not one of our earlier risers."

"He didn't put out his DND sign," Tiffany continued, enunciating each word precisely. "I assumed he wanted his room tidied. Therefore, I went in."

"Yes?" Rudley prompted.

"He was lying on his bed. It seems he had been ill. The vomit had dribbled from the corner of his mouth, and crusted in the creases of his neck. The front of his shirt was caked with it."

"I'll get an ambulance." Margaret reached for the phone.

"He's probably just had one too many," Rudley muttered. "I'll go down and take care of it." He came out from behind the desk, turned and bellowed, "Lloyd."

"Yes'm." Lloyd's voice came faintly from the other side of the wall.

"He's repairing some quarter round in the ballroom," Margaret said. "Do you think Mr. Arnold is going to be a problem?"

"I'm not afraid of Mr. Arnold, Margaret, but I may need Lloyd to help me haul him out of the mess."

Tiffany continued to stare at the desk top.

"Come along, dear," said Margaret. "We'll sit you down and get you a nice cup of tea."

Lloyd appeared with hammer in hand. "You were wanting me?"

"I was." Rudley headed for the door. "Come with me." Rudley glanced toward the lake as they came out onto the veranda. Norman's rowboat bobbed at the dock. Norman would be out as soon as he finished breakfast. The Sawchucks were making their way to the dock, followed by Tim, who had, apparently, been commandeered to help them board their rowboat.

"If Doreen would stop packing on the pounds, she wouldn't need two men to stuff her into the boat," Rudley said.

Lloyd giggled. "She has a big behind."

"She blames Gregoire's cooking," Rudley muttered. "You'd think he tied her down and force-fed her."

Rudley galloped across the lawn with Lloyd at his heels. He stopped at the Pines, hammered at the door. "If we make enough noise, he may wake up and mop up before we're forced to go in,"

Rudley said. He waited a minute, then banged on the door again. "Mr. Arnold." He called Mr. Arnold's name several times without response, then turned to Lloyd. "I'm afraid there's no way around it." He fished out his master key, opened the door. He stopped, stared.

Lloyd peered over Rudley's shoulder. "Don't smell so good in here."

Rudley suppressed the bile rising in his throat. "Forget the commentary, Lloyd." He edged toward the bed.

"Don't look like he's breathing," said Lloyd.

"Of course he's breathing," Rudley hissed. He took another step. "Mr. Arnold?"

"Don't look like he's going to answer," said Lloyd.

Rudley thrust two fingers into the side of Arnold's neck, turning his face away.

"Dead as a doornail," said Lloyd.

"Rudley" — Margaret looked up as Rudley barged into the lobby, followed by Lloyd — "is Mr. Arnold all right?"

Rudley paused. "No, he isn't, Margaret."

"Dead as a doornail," said Lloyd.

Margaret put a hand to her mouth. "Oh, dear. You didn't leave him by himself?"

Rudley took a deep breath. "Yes, we did. We closed the door so the coyotes wouldn't get him, and left. He's dead. He would have been just as dead if we'd stayed."

"All alone?"

"He won't be alone for long. I called the police from his cabin. We should hear sirens any minute now. Ambulances, police cruisers, evidence vans. Maybe even the volunteer fire department."

"Are you absolutely sure he's dead?"

"Trust me, Margaret, the man's dead."

"Why, this is terrible, Rudley."

He leaned against the desk, folded his arms. "Well, I don't know. No one particularly liked him. He was always in the middle of one unsavoury mess or another."

"Mrs. Millotte says he's a boob," Lloyd volunteered.

Rudley nodded. "Melba and I don't see eye to eye on many of the issues of the day, but her intuition about Arnold was impeccable."

The sound of sirens rose and fell as an ambulance and police car rushed past the front door.

"But, Rudley, what could have happened to him?"

"I imagine he had a heart attack. He was that sort of man — fleshy around the gills." He paused. "Although, I'm sure Brisbois will try to turn it into foul play. I don't know why he's so eager to have every death around here a murder."

"Probably because he's a homicide detective."

"There was vomit all over," said Lloyd.

"Oh, dear." Margaret started to move out from behind the desk. "I'll go down. We can't have Tiffany dealing with that."

Rudley stopped her. "Margaret, Brisbois will have the body fluids packaged up. He usually does. Lloyd and I will go in when he's through to see what needs to be done."

She squeezed his arm. "That's very gallant of you and Lloyd." She sighed. "You're taking this well."

Lloyd grinned. "Wasn't a minute ago."

Rudley glared at him, then sagged against the desk. "What a fine state of affairs for a wedding. Two dead bodies before the first 'I do'. Some brides would find that off-putting."

She nodded. "We should be grateful Miss Miller isn't one of them."

"Now, let me get this straight." Brisbois thumbed through his notes. "You went down there because Tiffany reported that Mr. Arnold was lying on his back, covered in vomit. Did she say he was dead?"

Rudley crossed his arms. "No. I think she's getting a little tired of making those announcements."

Brisbois shook his head. "He didn't respond to your knock, so you used your master key to get in."

"That's right." Rudley glowered. "Why do you have to rehash this? Do you think I'm going to tell you something different the second time?"

Brisbois gave him a long look. "You'd be surprised how often people do." He paused. "So you unlocked the door and saw him lying on the bed."

"Yes."

"Did you move him, roll him over?"

"No. I felt for a pulse. In his neck. That's all I did."

Brisbois flicked his pen. "When did you last see Mr. Arnold alive?"

"He was up for dinner last night. He stayed around for a while."

"How long?"

"I'm not sure. I believe he was in the ballroom for at least an hour."

"Is that his usual pattern?"

"No, he doesn't usually stay for the entertainment. He usually goes into town."

"Did he go into town last night?"

"I don't know."

"Did he have anything to drink at dinner?"

"You'll have to ask Tim. He had a glass of something in the ballroom."

"OK," Brisbois murmured. "Did he complain about being sick?"

"No, but he always looked unhealthy, if you ask me. With that red face, the man was a prime candidate for a heart attack or stroke."

"I guess he doesn't have to worry about that now," said Brisbois. He looked at Rudley, pen poised. "Did he have any visitors? Anybody come to see him while he was here?"

"Not that I'm aware of."

"Did you put any calls through to his cabin?"

"Not that I'm aware of."

"We'll check your telephone log."

"Then why did you bother asking?" Rudley fumed. "Are you through with me?"

"For now.

Rudley stamped off.

Brisbois sank into the chair, pushing back his hat. "The guy smelled like a distillery."

Creighton wrinkled his nose. "Booze mixed with a little eau de vomit."

"He gets drunk, passes out, chokes on his vomit."

Creighton shoved his hands into his pockets. "An experienced drinker like old Jack?"

Brisbois shrugged. "Maybe you have another theory?"

Chapter 14

The pathologist looked at Brisbois over his glasses. "I hope this is the last I see of you for a while."

Creighton chuckled.

"You too." The pathologist dropped into the creaking, cracked leather chair behind his desk, leafed through the file. "Hmm, what can I tell you? Your man was not in great shape. He had diabetes — poorly managed — coronary artery disease. Liver showed cirrhotic changes. He could have dropped dead at any time."

Brisbois shuffled his feet. "Are you saying he died of natural causes?"

"He choked on his vomit."

"He choked to death."

"Yes, set up by a gallon of booze and a whack of Benadryl."

Brisbois' forehead creased. "How much?"

"The levels suggest about ten capsules."

Brisbois stared at him. "Wouldn't you have to be awfully itchy to take ten capsules?"

The pathologist sat back. "I don't think it's something you'd do by accident." He reached for the file, pulled it into his lap. "There may be other substances involved. I won't know until I get the full tox screen. But Benadryl was the only drug in his possession so we ran that."

"Nothing for diabetes or heart?"

The pathologist shook his head. "That's all they brought in. His family doctor hasn't seen him in months. Their relationship soured, according to the doc, when he read him the riot act about the booze. He had Type 2 diabetes but he refused to take medication or make any modifications to his lifestyle. In denial, I guess."

Brisbois considered this. "So you're thinking suicide."

"Why not? His health was the pits. With blood sugars like his he was headed for a mess of trouble down the road. Amputations, blindness, kidney failure, you name it. Maybe he had financial troubles too. His clothes were top of the line but pretty well-worn, frayed at the cuffs and collar."

"He's a single guy," Brisbois said. "Divorced. Maybe his wife took care of those things."

"Could be," the pathologist conceded. "Or he couldn't afford the eighty-dollar shirts anymore and couldn't bring himself to shop at Sears."

Brisbois' eyes wandered to the pickled appendix on the desk. The label said *Jim's.* "Any evidence of foul play?"

The pathologist levered himself forward. "There're no signs anyone forced the stuff down his throat, although someone could have spiked the booze. I suppose that's up to you to figure out."

"Do you think he could have survived the combination if he hadn't vomited?"

"Possibly. With timely medical intervention."

Brisbois frowned. "If it wasn't accidental, say someone spiked the booze, wouldn't that be a little hard to get down?"

"Not if you're half-potted to begin with. If you think back to your student days, would you have noticed if someone slipped something into your drink?"

Creighton grinned. "I can think of times I might not have noticed if someone had slipped a dead toad into my drink."

"I never got that drunk," Brisbois murmured. He made a note. "So it's booze and Benadryl with the how and why to be determined."

"For now. I'll let you know if we get anything else on the tox screen."

"What do you think, Boss?" Creighton followed Brisbois into the hall, leaned against the wall as Brisbois paused to leaf through his notes.

"I think Arnold didn't strike me as the suicidal type."

"Like the doc said, money troubles."

"He didn't seem to be overly burdened by that. He was an entrepreneurial type. I think he could have got something going."

"His health was lousy," Creighton said. "And if he had diabetes, maybe he had ED. What do you think that would have done to a guy like Arnold?"

Brisbois shook his head. "A guy like Arnold would have had himself on Viagra. But I can't see suicide. He didn't strike me as introspective. I think he'd have to really hit the skids before he'd admit to having a serious problem. The way he acted around the Pleasant, you'd think he had the world by the tail." He turned toward the exit. "I want to do another walk-through at the Pines."

"Rudley's taking the latest better than I thought he would," said Creighton as they pulled into the Pleasant.

Brisbois climbed out of the passenger's seat, paused to stretch his back. "That's because he assumes the guy dropped dead of a heart attack."

They walked to the Pines. Officer Owens stood outside the yellow tape.

"How's it going?" Brisbois greeted.

"Everybody's stopped to offer their condolences, see what they could see," Owens said. "Otherwise, nothing."

"You keep a record of who came by?"

Owens held up his notebook. "And what they said."

"Good." Brisbois pushed open the door. He took a few steps inside, stopped and looked around.

The crime scene unit had completed its work.

"So," said Brisbois, "he was up at the inn until around nine."

"One of the guests, Mr. Oliver, thought he saw him near the dock around that time. Maybe he was thinking about drowning himself but lost his nerve."

"Yeah." Brisbois crossed the room, took a long look at the stripped bed. "Have you got a list of the stuff they took out of here?"

Creighton reached into his breast pocket, took out a folded sheet of paper, handed it to Brisbois

Brisbois studied the list. He went into the kitchen, looked into the cupboards, checked the garbage, then went into the bathroom. He checked through the medicine cabinet, came out, brow furrowed. Creighton watched as he got down on his hands and knees, and looked under the bed and bedside table. He continued his tour around the cabin, opening drawers, inspecting wastepaper baskets. Finally, he stopped and turned to Creighton.

"Know what isn't on that list?"

"Diana Krall's telephone number."

"The blister pack from the Benadryl." Brisbois pointed to an item on the list. "What's documented here is one package of Benadryl with two capsules missing. What does that mean?"

"The techs took an empty blister pack and forgot to document it."

"Or?" Brisbois prompted.

Creighton gestured to the disarray on the counter. "Arnold threw the empty blister pack into the garbage because he's such a neat guy."

Brisbois rocked back on his heels. "Or somebody else brought the Benadryl in and took the empty blister pack with them. Or maybe they emptied it first and just brought the pills in."

Creighton shook his head. "You're determined to make this a murder, aren't you?"

Brisbois raised his brows. "If forensics didn't take the blister pack, it's a reasonable supposition." He beckoned to Creighton. "Come on. There's something I want to check out."

Creighton wrinkled his nose. "I'll bet you're planning on diving into every garbage can on the place."

Brisbois gave him a cherubic smile. "Only half of them."

"Of course, I keep Benadryl in my medicine cabinet," said Rudley. "Don't you?"

"As a matter of fact, no," said Brisbois. "What do you keep it for?"

"In case someone gets into something they're allergic to. That happens often enough to warrant having some on hand."

"I keep a package handy," said Mr. Bole. "You never know when someone might need it."

Mrs. Sawchuck looked at Walter. They shook their heads in unison.

"We never keep Benadryl," said Walter.

"What do you do if you get dermatitis?" asked Brisbois, using the term he had heard bandied about after interviewing everyone on the premises.

"A little dab of hydrocortisone cream works quite nicely," said Walter.

Creighton checked back in with Brisbois.

"Half the people here have a few of those capsules," said Brisbois.

"No empty blister packs, though," said Creighton. "The paramedics didn't take any. Neither did our guys."

"Maybe it went out in the garbage."

Creighton gave Brisbois a look to kill. "I hope you're not suggesting we're going to root around in the county dump."

"We'll just have to check the orange bags," said Brisbois. "That's what they use around here."

"This is a new suit."

Brisbois regarded the light-grey summer-weight suit. "I see your point. I'll put Semple on it."

Rudley had been sorting through a stack of invoices when Brisbois posed his question. He tossed them into the air, exasperated. "Why in hell would I remove an empty package?" he said as the papers fluttered down around him.

"Because you were flustered," said Brisbois.

"I was not flustered."

"You'd just discovered Mr. Arnold, dead in one of your cabins. Why wouldn't you be flustered?"

Rudley drew himself up to his full height. "I'll have you know I was as cool as a cucumber."

Brisbois flipped through his notebook, gave Rudley a pointed look. "Interview with Mr. Lloyd Brawly." He commenced to read.

> Brisbois: Why did you and Mr. Rudley go to the Pines?
>
> Lloyd: Because Mr. Rudley said Tiffany saw Mr. Arnold lying in vomit.
>
> Brisbois: So when you and Mr. Rudley got to the Pines, was the door locked?
>
> Lloyd: Yes'm [sic].
>
> Brisbois: How did you get in?
>
> Lloyd: Mr. Rudley pounded for a while. But nobody answered so he used his key.
>
> Brisbois: So Mr. Rudley used his master key to open the door.
>
> Lloyd: Yes'm [sic].
>
> Brisbois: Who went in first?
>
> Lloyd: Mr. Rudley.
>
> Brisbois: And where were you?
>
> Lloyd: Just behind.
>
> Brisbois: What did you see?
>
> Lloyd: Mr. Arnold was lying on his back on the bed, and there was vomit all over him, and Mr. Rudley went over and stuck his fingers into his neck.
>
> Brisbois: And then?
>
> Lloyd: Mr. Rudley didn't believe he was dead, but I said, "He's as dead as a doornail".
>
> Brisbois: Go on.
>
> Lloyd: And Mr. Rudley said, "Oh, for crissakes."

Brisbois looked at Rudley. "He has a great knack for quoting you word for word. I mean, I've never heard Lloyd swear unless he's quoting you." He paused. "You sound a little flustered."

Rudley began to scoop up the invoices. "I wasn't delighted to see a dead body. But I wasn't put off enough to pick something up without knowing I had."

"Is that so?" Brisbois returned to his notes. "Listen to this."

Brisbois: *Then what?*

Lloyd: *Then Mr. Rudley said, "We've got to call an ambulance. Where's the damned phone?" And I said, "In your hand."*

Brisbois gave Rudley a there-you-see shrug. "If you didn't realize you had picked up the phone, how can you be sure you didn't pick up something else?"

Rudley clutched the loose invoices to his chest. "I know I didn't. Clearly, I picked up the phone as a natural subconscious reaction. In other words, my subconscious mind told me the next logical step would be to call for an ambulance. My subconscious mind wouldn't have any reason to tell me to pick up anything else."

Brisbois gave him a dubious look. "OK, who was at the Pines besides you and Lloyd? Between the time you called the ambulance and the first responders appeared?"

"Nobody."

"None of the guests poked their noses in to see what was going on?"

"The three bears dropped by, but left when they found we didn't have any honey."

"And you stayed with Mr. Arnold until the first responders arrived?"

"No."

"You left him alone?"

Rudley crossed his eyes. "He was dead."

"What I'm trying to get at is, is there a chance somebody could have got in between you leaving and the paramedics arriving?"

"No. I locked the door."

"Are you sure?"

Rudley gritted his teeth. "Yes. We never leave a cabin without locking the door. I had to go down after and open it up for them."

Brisbois smiled, snapped his notebook shut. "I think that's enough for now."

Brisbois rejoined Creighton. "Anything from Semple?"

Creighton grinned. "Yeah. Only four bags came in from the Pleasant in the last week. Lloyd confirms that number."

"Not much for an inn."

"They compost and recycle almost everything."

"OK."

"Semple found two empty blister packs in those bags," Creighton said. "One was from Zantac and the other one was from Terazosin. That's something for blood pressure. Walter takes it."

Brisbois jammed his hands into his pockets. "It has to be somewhere."

Creighton thought for a moment. "What if there wasn't a blister pack? What if Arnold emptied the Benadryl into something else? He could have discarded the packaging days ago. Maybe weeks."

Brisbois sighed. "I suppose he could have, although I don't see why he would." He pushed his chair back from the desk, stood up. "We'll check with the paramedics again, make sure they didn't drop it in with their gear by mistake. But I can't see them forgetting if they found the empty package. Those hot dogs always want to be the heroes. They'd be looking for cause of death. If they spotted the empty Benadryl package, they'd know it was significant." He paced around the room, stopped. "If somebody brought the pills in, they could have discarded the packaging anywhere."

"So you're set on the idea somebody fed him the pills."

"Yeah, I am. The only question is how did they do it?"

"The old-fashioned way. They spiked his booze."

"It had to have happened after he left the inn," Brisbois mused. "I can't see someone doing that in front of witnesses."

"Anything's possible."

"Yeah, but if someone wanted him dead, they wouldn't want him to collapse at the inn. Somebody'd call an ambulance. They'd truck him off to the hospital, and, chances are, he'd survive."

"Maybe they didn't want him dead. Maybe somebody just wanted to play a joke on him."

Brisbois shook his head. "That would require extreme stupidity. I don't think anybody here has that much."

Creighton flopped down onto the settee. "OK, if someone did it on purpose, what's the motive?"

"We haven't found anybody who liked him so far."

Creighton nodded. "What about the Hopper family? It must be a sore spot with them, knowing Arnold tried to hustle Evelyn just before she died."

"Yeah, that would eat at me." Brisbois picked up his hat. "We'll talk to them."

"But you're not too convinced."

"I wouldn't rule anything out." He stood, put his hat on, sat down, took it off again. "Let's just recap what we've got on Arnold. The guy had allergies. He used Benadryl. Several people here saw him take the pills at least once. The package in the evidence bag had two pills missing. Doc says he had five times that amount in his system. But we didn't find any empty boxes or blister packs."

Creighton ticked the possibilities off on his fingers. "They forgot to add it to the list. Somebody misplaced it. It got stuck on the bottom of Lloyd's big muddy work boot. If that's what happened, it could be anywhere within fifty square miles."

Brisbois dismissed this. "Lloyd wouldn't go inside with muddy boots on. Tiffany's got him well-trained."

Creighton took a paper from his pocket. "Arnold's overdrawn by two thousand in his chequing account. His savings account went south a long time ago. I don't know if the bank he had it in still exists. He's got fifteen thousand on his credit cards. He's got a third mortgage on his house."

Brisbois craned his neck to look at the sheet in Creighton's hand. "What does it say about the business? He must have some assets there."

Creighton shook his head. "Not much. Two half-ton trucks — both over five years old. He and his wife had a nasty breakup.

She was the business manager. She put in the bids, ran everything. He knew the construction end."

"Did she say why they broke up? Another woman?"

"There were lots of women. Mainly it was the booze."

"Makes you feel kind of sorry for the guy."

Creighton folded the paper, tucked it into his breast pocket. "If these financial records were mine, I might do myself in." He paused. "Maybe he dropped the packaging for the Benadryl into the sink. The cardboard got wet. Maybe the blister pack wasn't intact. He was afraid the pills might get wet so he popped them out and put them into a glass. So last night, he took the ones from the glass and two from the package."

Brisbois shifted. "Yeah, I agree it could happen like that. Still, it doesn't make sense. I mean, if he had some in the glass and he took them, why would he bother opening a new package and just take two? Why wouldn't he take a bunch? I mean, he wouldn't know what a lethal dose was, especially if he was as drunk as his alcohol levels say he was."

Creighton shrugged. "But maybe he did. We can't assume every dead body we find around here is foul play."

"They have been so far," Brisbois grumbled. He snapped his fingers. "I know somebody who might be able to shed some light on this."

Tiffany was behind the desk when Brisbois and Creighton entered the lobby.

"Detectives," she greeted. "I'm afraid Mr. Rudley isn't here."

Brisbois removed his hat. "Actually, you're the one we want to talk to."

She gave him her full attention.

"You tidied up Mr. Arnold's cabin every day."

"Yes."

"Did you empty the garbage?"

"Of course. Every day."

"Do you remember seeing an empty blister pack? You know those foil things they pack pills in?"

She thought for a moment. "I don't remember anything like that. But you must understand I take pains not to notice what's in the guests' garbage."

"Incriminating stuff?"

"Liquor bottles. Personal items. Some of them very personal."

"I see."

She shook her head. "I should say I try not to dwell on what I find in the guests' garbage. I do pay attention. In case someone has discarded something they didn't intend to. For example, Mrs. Sawchuck dropped her watch into the basket by mistake. I noticed it before it was discarded."

"I imagine she was glad of that."

"She was." Tiffany paused. "With Mr. Arnold, it was hard not to notice his garbage. Most of it didn't make it into the bin. There were usually bits of paper, tissues, packaging, things like that on the floor around it. But I don't remember seeing a blister pack."

Brisbois thought for a moment. "OK. Do you remember seeing any pills lying around loose, in a glass or a saucer, something like that?"

She shook her head. "No, I don't remember seeing anything like that. I'm sorry."

Brisbois gave her a smile. "You've been helpful. Thanks, Tiffany."

He went out onto the veranda. Creighton followed.

"She didn't see anything."

Creighton jingled his keys. "OK, what about this? He puts the pills into a glass. He puts the glass into the medicine cabinet."

Brisbois didn't answer. He folded his arms over the railing, looked down to where Norman lay snoring in his rowboat. Mr. Bole was at the dock, manipulating a model boat with a remote control.

Creighton laughed. "Maybe Bole's doing *Mutiny on the Bounty* next."

"Arnold went into town every night after supper," Brisbois said. "Except his last night. That night he stayed around for part of the entertainment. He went out, wandered around the dock. Then what? Why didn't he go into town?"

"Because there was a mob of women waiting to lynch him?" Creighton shrugged. "Maybe he was depressed. He stayed around the inn, thinking being part of the crowd might buck him up. It didn't. He goes back to his cabin, takes an inventory of his life, including reviewing his bankbook — which was a big mistake. He decides it isn't worth it. He takes a handful of Benadryl, washes it down with a bottle of booze, and goes to sleep. He doesn't wake up."

Brisbois hunched his shoulders. "He didn't leave a note. He didn't make any phone calls. People usually try to say goodbye to someone. He had two kids."

Creighton shrugged. "Yeah, but that's if he'd been mulling it over for a while. Maybe it was an impulse thing. Maybe he wasn't even sure he wanted to die. He just wanted to get some relief, get away for a while."

Brisbois gave him a sour look. "Have you been reading that damned Durkheim book again?"

"I read it for that course. Suicide is a risk-taking deal. You can't guarantee you're going to die. Look at the guy who put the gun to his head and didn't do anything but blow off his ear and singe his toupee."

Brisbois' mouth turned down. He didn't relish murder; he simply hated the idea of suicide. Hated the idea someone could think there was so little use in living that they'd do something like that to themselves. There was always something to live for, wasn't there? Something to get you over the hump? "I don't think guys like Arnold commit suicide," he said. "No introspection."

"I don't think you have to be a deep thinker to commit suicide," said Creighton. "You've just got to find yourself in a shitload of trouble with no way out."

"They vacuumed for trace."

Creighton nodded. "They did everything they were supposed to do. But I don't know how much good that will do. With everybody back and forth, brushing against everything. Tiffany probably transfers a ton of trace every time she dusts."

Brisbois gave him a gloomy nod. "Talk to the wife again. Get a list of everybody he knew. We'll work the phones. Find out everything we can about this guy." He thrust his hands into his pockets, then returned his gaze to the lake. "Can you think of anything that would make you want to commit suicide?"

"Maybe if I was two hundred years old and had lost both my legs and couldn't get a date. Even then, if there were a few good-looking nurses around..."

Brisbois frowned. "You wouldn't worry about your soul?"

Creighton gave him a surprised look. "Hey, I was brought up in the United Church."

Brisbois turned, gave him a bleak look.

"Look, Boss, if you don't mind me saying, you are on a wild-goose chase here. You've turned the inn upside down, made Semple dirty his shoes. For what? The guy committed suicide. His health was lousy. He was in financial free fall. The last woman he made a move on threw an Old-Fashioned in his face. You've seen suicides before."

"Yeah." Brisbois left the railing, headed down the steps, said without turning, "And I've never liked them."

Chapter 15

Terri Hopper jumped up from her chair at the table in the interrogation room and ran to stand by the window. Creighton took a step toward her, then resumed his position against the wall. Brisbois tapped his notebook, waited until she returned to her seat.

"I don't know what you want," she said through tears. "My mother's dead and now you're acting as if Rico or Dad or I killed Mr. Arnold. Rico and I weren't even at the Pleasant last night. We were with Dad all night. He hasn't left the house since he came home from the hospital. He's practically comatose from the pills they put him on."

Brisbois abandoned his notebook, sat back in his chair. "Look at it from our point of view, Terri. You had good reason to want to get back at Arnold. He put the moves on your mother at the hotel. He could have been the last person to see her alive — apart from the murderer. Maybe you suspect he killed her."

She gritted her teeth. "Maybe he did."

Brisbois did not respond. He sat, watching her, absently stroking his cheek with his thumb.

"We didn't go near him," she said. "Rico and I made dinner for Dad. Then we spent most of the evening grooming the horses, just spending time with them." She bent her head. "It's hard for them with Mom gone." A tear rolled down her cheek. "Dad might as well be gone."

Brisbois sat forward, opened his notebook, flipped back a few pages. "You know, Terri, I have to tell you, in a murder case, you can't hold anybody above suspicion."

"Dad can't even find his way to the yard," she murmured. "Rico and I are afraid to leave him alone."

Brisbois flicked his pen. "Is there anybody who can verify you were home last night?"

She shrugged. "We talked to some people on the phone."

He made a note. "Land line?"

She looked hopeful as he wrote this down. "Yes, we talked to Mr. Tiggan, the farrier."

"When was that?"

"Around six." She mopped up tears with the back of her hand. "We called Rico's mom after supper, around eight. Aunt Joan called somewhere after nine. We were watching television."

"Baseball game?"

"No, that didn't start until ten. They were playing in Seattle. We were watching CNN. After we talked to Aunt Joan, we washed the dishes. Then we went down to check the horses. Then we came up to watch the baseball game."

Brisbois wrote all of this down. He believed the phone calls would check out but he would follow up for the sake of being thorough. In truth, he didn't think Terri or her dad or Rico had anything to do with Jack Arnold's death. No one had seen any of them around the Pleasant. Still, something wasn't right. Terri and Rico had a hard time looking him in the eye. He finished his notes, made some doodles in the margins. "Terri," he said without warning, "I think you're holding something back on us. In fact, I know you are."

She flushed.

"First, you lied to us about your whereabouts the night your mother died." He put up a hand to stop her protests. "I know you didn't want anybody to know you were staying with Rico. But you were being questioned in a murder investigation. That should have been the least of your worries."

She gulped.

"Detective Creighton and I may not be Einstein, but we're pretty good at figuring out things." He turned to Creighton. "Detective, could you go over what we found when we were looking around?"

Creighton pushed himself off the wall, took out his notebook, and came to sit at the table beside Brisbois. "A couple of things puzzled us. The pathologist believes the shovel we took from the stable was exactly like the instrument that injured your mother and opened that cut on Ned."

"Except there was no blood on that shovel and nothing from the barn — straw and oats and so forth." Brisbois gestured to Creighton to continue.

"But what the shovel we took from the stable did have on it was ordinary garden soil."

Brisbois looked to Terri. "Now, that seems strange."

"Our team took a good look around," Creighton said. "And there wasn't another shovel like it on the place. There was a snow shovel — that was in the garden shed — but there wasn't any shovel anywhere that looked as if it had been used in the stables."

"And that doesn't make sense," said Brisbois.

"Whoever killed Mom took it," she said.

Brisbois forehead wrinkled. "Now, that would make sense. But the shovel in the stable with nothing on it but garden soil, that doesn't make any sense at all."

She studied the table.

Brisbois closed his notebook. "Here's what I think happened. You came home. Your mother wasn't there. Your father was vague about her whereabouts. His clothes were dirty. You knew your parents weren't getting along. You went down to see the horses. You saw the blood on the shovel and on the door frame. You got a bad feeling. You got rid of the shovel. But you thought it would look funny if there wasn't a shovel in the stable because there always was. And there were probably people who could say there was. Maybe your Aunt Joan. Maybe the farrier. So you took the shovel from the garden shed." He looked at her pale face. "Now that was a bit of overthinking on your part. Because if you'd just disposed of the shovel, we would have assumed the killer took it with him."

She moistened her lips. "I thought…"

"We know what you thought. You thought your father had done something to your mother, and you were trying to help him out."

She took a deep breath. "Yes."

"Where's the shovel?"

She moistened her lips. "In the quarry. I wrapped it in a blanket and put it in the back of my car, on the floor. Nobody looked in my car. When I had a chance, I threw it in the quarry."

"Where?"

"It's off the back road about two miles away. It's flooded."

Brisbois nodded. "OK, tell us the story."

She collected her thoughts. "I saw the blood on the shovel. I thought maybe one of the horses had stepped on a mouse. I washed it down. Then when I found out about what had happened to Mom I thought you would think Dad had killed her, so I threw it away."

"Did you wash the handle down too?"

She nodded reluctantly.

He studied his notes, then looked up at her.

She met his noncommittal gaze. "Am I in trouble?"

Terri had left. Brisbois sat at the desk, staring at his notes, shaking his head.

"I think she's in trouble," Creighton said finally.

Brisbois nodded. "The only question is how much. By the time they fish that shovel out of that quarry, it won't be worth much. Especially after all that cleaning." He pitched his pen across the table. "There were probably fingerprints."

"I guess that would be too easy."

"Damn." Brisbois gave his earlobe an irritated tug. "If Carl killed his wife, Terri would be an accomplice after the fact."

"And that would be a shame," Creighton said, "because she's kind of a nice kid and she reminds you of your youngest daughter." He gave Brisbois a playful poke in the shoulder. "You're such an old softie."

"Soft in the head's more like it," Brisbois muttered. He closed the notebook, stuffed it into his pocket, hauled himself up to retrieve his pen. "OK, let's reconvene this party at the quarry."

Brisbois and Creighton stood by as the divers entered the quarry.

"That water looks cold," said Creighton.

"It's like deep well water," said Brisbois. He leaned back against the car. "This thing keeps getting more complicated." He frowned. "You know what's bugging me?"

"Nope."

"Nobody has a good explanation about what Evelyn Hopper was doing in the bar that night."

"Maybe somebody stood her up. Maybe she came home, saw Carl flaked out, drooling on the furniture, couldn't stand the sight of him, went into town for a drink. Nick saw her on the dock. Maybe she was supposed to meet Alva, but he thought his wife was onto him and chickened out."

"I suppose." Brisbois shrugged. "It would have been nice to have this thing wrapped up before the wedding."

Creighton sipped his coffee. "Are you bringing Mary?"

Brisbois gave him a surprised look. "Of course. She's really looking forward to it. What about you? Who are you bringing?"

"I haven't decided."

"You're leaving it kind of late."

Creighton shrugged. "Maybe I'll ask Petrie."

"Petrie doesn't like you."

"So what? She looks good."

Brisbois gave him a smug smile. "I hear she's asked Vance."

Creighton hooted. "Vance. He's skinny, half-bald, and he's got that cheesy moustache. Give me a break."

"He's a nice guy."

Creighton smirked. "So that's it. She wants a nice guy."

Brisbois smiled. "Just kidding. Petrie likes you."

"She does?"

"Sure. She just doesn't want to go out with you." Brisbois lit a cigarette before continuing. "Your problem, Creighton, is you're always looking for the wrong thing. You like the idea of some companionship — when you want it — but you're afraid of commitment. That could lead to marriage and that would cramp your style."

"Maybe."

"Where you're wrong is in thinking marriage is going to limit you. Marriage makes things better."

Creighton waited patiently.

"Married men live longer. They eat better, get regular checkups. Their wives keep them up to date. You get somebody to share things with, somebody to pick you up. I'd have a tough time doing my job sometimes if it weren't for Mary."

"I think I've heard this speech before."

"I just don't want to see you hanging out in bars when you're seventy."

Creighton gave him a long look. "I think you married guys don't like single guys like me because we scare you."

"How do you figure that?"

"You worry you're missing something. Maybe you feel tempted."

Brisbois gave him an annoyed look and sank his cigarette into the dregs of his coffee.

Chapter 16

"Well, Rudley?" Margaret looked up apprehensively as Rudley entered the lobby.

Rudley paused, leaned against the desk. "Lloyd has left to take Mr. Arnold's things to the train. The Pines has been scrubbed, aired out. New mattress, fresh linens. When the Franklins check in next week, they won't suspect a thing."

"I'm glad, Rudley." She came around the desk, gave him a peck on the cheek. "I think I'll grab a bite. Do you want anything?"

"Maybe later." He went behind the desk, glanced at the newspaper. "War in the Middle East, forest fires in California," he muttered. "I'm glad we're not in the headlines for a change." He smiled, did a two-step, hummed a few bars of "I've Got the World on a String." With the situation at the Pines behind him, the future looked rosy. And why not? Lovely wedding to look forward to. Wonderful girl, Miss Miller. The situation had looked dicey for a while, but everything was coming together as they had hoped. The police tapes were down. Detectives Brisbois and Creighton would be out from underfoot soon — none too soon. And the Pines was back to normal.

He paused. In spite of the reputation of the Pleasant, he'd never had a guest ask if someone had died in the accommodation they were about to occupy. Perhaps the cheerful hominess of the rooms made it impossible to believe that anything heinous had happened there.

So the mattress had gone to the dump. Arnold's personal effects had gone to his estate. He could safely say there was nothing left of Jack Arnold at the Pleasant.

He frowned. It was unfortunate that it was so easy to erase a human being from a place. A little Lysol, a set of crisp white sheets, the clean forest fragrance through an open window.

He remembered working at the Baltimore, where every room greeted a visitor as if it had been constructed for him alone. He grinned, wondering if those two old nuns could have imagined that the room they shared had been occupied by a salesman from Niagara Falls who had smuggled in a different lady of the evening three nights in a row. He thought for a moment, shook his head. Never.

Brisbois reminded himself to stop at the dry cleaners to pick up his blue suit. Miss Miller and Mr. Simpson had indicated in their invitation that guests were to come as they wished, but Mary had convinced him that it would be disrespectful not to wear his best suit. He wasn't sure what she would be wearing, but whatever it was, she would look good. Mary hadn't gained an ounce since they were married. He wished he could say the same for himself. Too many fast-food meals, not enough exercise. He sighed. Too much stress.

His hand reached compulsively for his notebook, fluttered back to the wheel. He hated this case.

Someone had clipped Mrs. Hopper on the head. The spade which might have done it was useless as evidence. He wished Terri Hopper had put a little more thought into what she was doing before she cleaned it and dumped it into the quarry. Carl Hopper's prints on the shovel would hardly have been incriminating. Not only had she destroyed evidence, she had not succeeded in making her father look less culpable.

Carl could have done it. Jack Arnold could have done it. Five hundred other people could have killed Evelyn Hopper who, as it turned out, was a nasty person. It was always easier to focus on a case when you liked the victim.

"I think Carl Hopper killed his wife," he said out loud. It felt good to say that. The wife was fooling around. He was having trouble with his writing. He stood to lose everything — his wife, his home, his horses, his security and peace of mind. He was a quiet guy, the kind of guy to whom home and hearth were everything, and she was going to take it all away. He reached for his cigarettes, paused to take the corner before lighting up. He believed Nick Anderson's assessment that Evelyn had been having an affair with Jim Alva was correct. But the guy had an alibi for the night of the murder.

Besides, what motive would Alva have for killing Evelyn? He took a deep drag from his cigarette, flicked the ashes out the window. Unless she was making noises about telling his wife.

A car towing a boat passed him. He couldn't remember the last time he'd gone fishing. He returned his thoughts to Evelyn Hopper. If she'd had one fling, she could have had others. Maybe with somebody she didn't have on the books. He gripped the steering wheel harder than necessary. They'd go over her appointment book again. Maybe the gaps would tell them something.

He shook his head. Now he was thinking it wasn't Carl who killed her. And it wasn't Jim Alva. It was some mystery man, someone who had been very discreet.

He pushed his hat back, wondered what had brought Carl and Evelyn together in the first place. They said opposites attracted. He wasn't sure about that. He and Mary enjoyed a lot of the same things, thought the same way about many things.

He thought of Creighton and chuckled. Creighton was a dedicated bachelor, terrified of marriage. He made sure that everyone knew he wasn't interested in getting serious. Brisbois wondered if he would find anyone to go to the wedding with him.

Then there was poor Owens who, apparently, was in Tiffany's bad books for hunting. I think I'd give up that for Tiffany, he thought. He didn't understand why a guy like Owens was so devoted to the sport. He had no interest in it himself.

He rubbed his forehead. The case had too many threads, all running in different directions. He needed a clear eye. Maybe if he went over the evidence with Miss Miller... He struck the steering wheel with the heel of his hand. What was he thinking?

He sat back, relaxed as the twisting road gave way to a straightaway. Evelyn Hopper and Jack Arnold were dead. Jack Arnold had had an unfortunate encounter with Evelyn. Ergo, he killed her, then committed suicide out of remorse. He was in the vicinity. Lloyd had washed the evidence off his shoes. It was that simple.

"*You know it's never that simple, Detective.*"

"Maybe it is this time, Miss Miller.

In his imagination, she smiled at him, then disappeared.

Chapter 17

On the morning of the wedding, not a soul at the Pleasant slept in. Guests and staff were up at dawn, flitting about the inn and the grounds, some busy with preparations, others busy getting in the way.

Rudley waited until the lobby was relatively quiet, then nipped into the kitchen for a croissant and coffee. He returned to the front desk, putting his coffee and croissant down on the newspaper, forgetting he had spread the newspaper across the ledger. The plate tipped, spilling the coffee and knocking the croissant onto the floor. He dove for it as Albert romped up, wagging his tail. Rudley grabbed the croissant, stood up, smacking his head on the edge of the desk.

"Goddamn."

Tim leaned over the desk. "It's yours. You beat him to it."

"Not before he got his tongue on it." Rudley ceded the croissant to Albert, who ambled back to the rug.

Tim took a long look at Rudley. "If you don't mind me saying so, you look as if you shaved with Gregoire's potato peeler."

"I was in a hurry," Rudley muttered.

"I could get the makeup kit."

Rudley glowered. "It'll be fine." He paused, stiffening at the sound of a motor. "What was that?"

"Must be the laundryman."

"What the hell?" Rudley dashed out from behind the counter, ran down the veranda steps, waving and yelling at the laundryman.

"What in hell are you doing here at this hour of the morning?" He ran around the truck, searching the ground, distracted.

Tim had followed Rudley out into the yard. He looked at him, bewildered.

"Aha." Rudley bent and picked up something.

"Mr. Rudley." The laundryman trotted toward him.

Rudley turned on him. "What in hell are you doing here" — he shifted the object to one hand, peered at his watch — "at six-thirty in the morning?"

The laundryman straightened his cap. "And what are you doing with a bullfrog in your hand at six-thirty in the morning?"

Rudley ignored him. He turned back toward the inn, handing the bullfrog off to Tim.

"What do you want me to do with him, Boss?"

"Escort him back to the swamp." Rudley charged up the steps.

The laundryman followed. "Would Mrs. Rudley be around?"

Rudley glared at him. "Not at the moment."

The laundryman sighed. "I'm afraid we have an unfortunate situation. That's why I'm early. I wanted you to be advised of it as soon as possible."

Rudley slammed his fist into the desk, slopping coffee over the ledger. "I knew it. You botched the linen order."

The laundryman shook his head. "No, that's not it."

"You've lost something." Rudley thought for a moment, raised a triumphant finger. "I know. The serviettes. Did you know those damned things were brought directly from Ireland?"

"That's very informative, Mr. Rudley," the laundryman said. "But that's not it."

Rudley gripped the edge of the desk until his knuckles turned white. "You've put a stain on my formal shirt."

The laundryman smiled. "You're getting a little warmer."

Rudley glowered. "You've stained Margaret's gown. You've stained the bride's gown. You've ripped the seat out of the groom's pants."

"Nothing was ripped or stained. As you know, Mr. Rudley, we have never ripped or stained any of your items."

"Out with it," said Rudley.

The laundryman paused, pursed his lips, then said carefully, "There was a fire."

"A fire?"

"In the dry-cleaning section."

"You mean our things were burned?"

"Melted. The fire was confined to a single row of hangers, but everything on it was singed or melted. Nothing recoverable, I'm afraid."

Rudley braced his hands against the desk, levered himself forward. "How in hell am I supposed to tell the wedding party on the morning of the nuptials that their clothes have melted?"

"You could say someone died," the laundryman said. "I've found people tend to be good sports in the wake of tragedy."

"Now, that's a fine way to start a married life," Rudley said. "Knowing someone perished trying to save your duds."

"I'm afraid I have nothing better to suggest," said the laundryman. "You and your guests will be reimbursed in full, of course."

"Of course," Rudley muttered.

"Well," said the laundryman. "I suppose I'll be seeing you later."

"Later?"

"The wedding. The young couple was gracious enough to invite me — owing to my attentiveness to their special needs."

"Gracious," Rudley muttered.

He shooed the laundryman away, pulled out a bottle of Chivas Regal. He squeezed a cigarette from the package of Benson and Hedges in the drawer, lit it. "I think I could be forgiven a few vices in the wake of this most recent development," he told Albert. He smiled a jaunty smile. "I never could tolerate that suit. Formal wear is all very good for dance but when you're just standing around it makes you look like a damned manikin." Simpson and Miss Miller had found their wedding outfits at a rummage sale. He admired their good sense. He stood for a moment, spewing smoke through his nostrils. How to tell the wedding party... He hoped everyone would be as reasonable as he.

"I'm terribly sorry to tell you this," Rudley finished.

Bonnie Lawrence uttered a mournful cry, clasped her head in her hands. "This is a tragedy."

Rudley glanced toward Miss Miller who was rolling her eyes. "The sinking of the *Titanic* was a tragedy, Mrs. Lawrence," he said. "This is merely unfortunate."

She regarded him with round, glistening eyes. "Unfortunate? Mr. Rudley, how can you be so insensitive?"

"Practice?" Tim suggested.

"A woman's wedding day is the most important day of her life," Bonnie cried. "How could that establishment be so careless?"

Rudley pulled a long face. "I heard a rumour the proprietor may have died."

"And there isn't time to get anything from the shops. Why didn't they telephone us immediately instead of waiting to send that man around… when it happened…when did it happen? If we'd known immediately, we might have been able to dash off to Ottawa…" Bonnie stopped, breathless.

"They probably had to put the fire out, call an ambulance, that sort of thing," said Rudley. He shook his head at Miss Miller, who stood behind Bonnie, mouthing, "Did someone really die?'"

"What will we do?" Bonnie shrieked.

Rudley thought for a moment, then brightened. "We'll leave it to Margaret. She'll come up with something." He cleared his throat, bellowed, "Margaret? Could you come here?"

She came out from the kitchen. "What's the matter, Rudley?"

"The laundry caught fire," Tim said. "The wedding outfits were destroyed."

Her jaw dropped.

"I told everyone not to worry, Margaret," Rudley said. "I told them you would know how to handle the situation."

Margaret paused, took in Bonnie's tear-stained face. "Of course," she said. "No need to worry. We'll come up with something."

"There" — Gregoire stepped back, gazed at his creation — "what do you think about that?"

Tim stared. "I have to say that is truly impressive."

Gregoire drew himself up to his full height. "At The School of Creative Culinary Design, I was awarded first prize for my wedding cakes — for presentation, for innovation, for texture, moisture, and, of course, for deliciousness."

"Maybe this will make up for the debacle with the outfits."

Gregoire rolled his eyes. "I hear Mrs. Lawrence is practically having a stroke over that."

Tim lowered his voice. "I actually heard Mr. Lawrence tell her to shut up about the damned clothes. Those were his words."

Gregoire took a turn around his creation. "Mr. Lawrence is not a gracious man. Bonnie Lawrence is a noodle brain but she made a big effort." He wiped his brow. "God knows I know that."

"Maybe the wedding ceremony will soften him up."

"I hope you are right," said Gregoire. "It is not nice to see someone treated like that, even if you think they have no priorities and brains like birds."

Tim selected a croissant, added a generous amount of peach butter. "I'm glad you have some of these left over. The guests are so excited about the wedding, half of them couldn't eat breakfast."

Gregoire took in his cake, gave a sigh of satisfaction. "They are saving themselves for the wedding buffet. They will go through that like locusts." He paused. "Maybe the wedding ceremony will improve Officer Owens' fortunes too."

Tim checked the fruit salad. "I think he would improve his chances if he stopped shooting everything in sight."

"Everyone must have his hobbies, I suppose," said Gregoire. "Tiffany should look at the hunting as one of those things they disagree about and let it go at that." He swept up his apron, blotted his forehead. "I have to say, if Tiffany continues to be so demanding, she will end up with the only one she approves of."

Tim raised his brows.

"Herself," said Gregoire.

Margaret came in, carrying a threadbare suit jacket, a pair of chinos, and an off-white shirt. "What do you think?"

"I think that outfit would go over very well at the lumberman's ball," said Tim. "Provided they held it in the woods."

Margaret sighed. "Herb was quite taken with the three-piece pinstripe. But since it burned, he won't wear anything but his own clothes. I'm afraid these are the best he has. But at least they're clean and pressed." She gave the shirt a doubtful look. "I think this might have been white at one time, but it's the best I could do. I was able to get the grass stains out of the neckerchief. It has a rather nice pattern. Quite dressy. I'll see if he'll let me fix it up as an ascot."

Tim tittered. "Now he'll look as if he was on his way to the lumberman's ball and ran into minor British royalty."

"I think you did a good job to turn a pig's ear into a purse," said Gregoire.

"He could have attended the wedding in a burlap sack — Miss Miller and Mr. Simpson would have thought nothing of it — but it's important for him to look the best he can." She took another look at the ensemble. "I'm going to see if Rudley has found that oxblood belt."

Miss Miller was at the desk, chatting with Rudley, when Margaret arrived in the lobby.

"Everything is going according to plan," Miss Miller announced. "I've kept the parents away from the local newspapers." She glanced around. "I've managed to escape Bonnie. She has some extravagant ideas for my hair."

"I think I've got Mrs. Lawrence under control," Rudley said. "I've commissioned her to write a poem to be read at the end of the reception and I've sent a complimentary bottle of champagne to her cabin. That should give her a good headache and, perhaps, keep her out of commission for a few hours."

"I hate to think how she'll react when she sees the wedding outfits."

"I think they're charming," said Miss Miller.

"I'm afraid I couldn't persuade Herb to wear a period costume," said Margaret. "I did the best I could with his things. I was thinking that oxblood belt of yours, Rudley, would be a good match with his outfit."

"I imagine a piece of binder twine would suffice."

"Be nice, Rudley."

Miss Miller's gaze fell on the neckerchief. "That neckerchief doesn't look very Herb."

"He probably got it from a bin at the church basement."

Miss Miller continued to stare at the neckerchief.

"Is anything wrong, dear?" Margaret asked.

Miss Miller shook her head, "No, I just thought it looked familiar."

"Perhaps you saw one like it in the shops."

Miss Miller started to say something, then smiled and turned toward the stairs. "I'd better drop in on Mother. She's dying to see the dress."

"Yes, dear."

"She's beside herself."

"I'll send up a bottle of white."

"That might help."

"Margaret, we're going to have everyone half-potted before the ceremony starts," Rudley said.

"Sometimes that's for the best." Margaret consulted her list. "I think we've done it, Rudley. I've telephoned the Reverend Pendergast to confirm Lloyd will be picking him up. The wedding clothes are ready. The cake is a work of art. You've taken care of Mrs. Lawrence." She patted him on the arm. "That was chivalrous of you."

He smiled a lopsided smile. "I'm a veritable knight in shining armour."

She dropped the list to the desk with satisfaction. "Rudley, we've done it."

"Don't we always?"

"It will be perfect." She gave him a hug. "Unforgettable."

Chapter 18

Rudley moved closer to Margaret, said in a hoarse whisper, "Margaret, that man's voice is like nails on a blackboard. I thought men of the cloth were supposed to be soothing."

She shushed him. "Be nice, Rudley."

Reverend Pendergast plodded along. Miss Miller's attention wandered. She turned her head, let her gaze drift over the crowd.

Tim stood to one side with Tiffany, Gregoire, and Lloyd, then Officer Petrie, Officer Vance, Detective Creighton, Officer Owens, the Phipps-Walkers, the Sawchucks, Detective Brisbois, and Mary.

"Do you, Edward Simpson…"

Simpson turned to Elizabeth. "I do." He paused, then repeated in a stage whisper to get her attention, "I do."

She smiled, distracted.

"And do you, Elizabeth Miller…"

Miss Miller continued to scan the gathering. Her gaze fell on Herb. She tilted her head, frowned.

"The reverend is asking if you want to marry me," Edward whispered.

She turned to him, smiled. "Of course, I do, Edward." She returned her attention to the guests.

Reverend Pendergast sighed when he heard *I do*. "Thank God, that's over," he said.

Simpson's forehead crimped. "I now pronounce you," he mouthed.

Reverend Pendergast chuckled. "Oh, it's not over. Of course. Pardon me. I now pronounce you man and wife."

Mr. Bole hit the keys. Cheers erupted from the audience.

"Isn't this wonderful, Rudley?"

"Wonderful, Margaret. The damned man has forgotten about signing the marriage certificate." Rudley waved to get the minister's attention, made a gesture to signify writing.

The reverend gave him an apologetic wave, took a folder from the table behind him.

"Now that would have been a fine state of affairs," said Rudley. "If they hadn't signed the registry."

Margaret squeezed his arm. "You've saved the day. They would have been off in the woods without a licence."

"I doubt if that would have put a damper on their activities, Margaret."

"Be nice, Rudley."

"I don't know about you, Margaret, but I think the modern mores do take the mystery out of the ceremony."

"Nonsense. Couples have been cohabiting without benefit of clergy since Adam and Eve."

"We didn't." He paused, smiled a jaunty smile. "Although I could have been persuaded."

"We were delighted when Edward and Elizabeth told us they were to marry." Mrs. Simpson cast a loving eye toward the buffet.

"Spirited girl," Mr. Simpson said. "Does our son the world of good. We were so worried Edward might marry someone like himself and have a perfectly boring life."

Mrs. Miller helped herself to a glass of punch. "Elizabeth needs someone like Edward," she told Detective Brisbois. "She's impulsive. She needs a steadying influence."

"She's a dynamo," said Mr. Simpson. He glanced to where Elizabeth Miller stood, talking to Herb. "But she has a tender heart." He leaned toward Detective Brisbois, whispered, "Much like Mrs. Simpson."

Brisbois smiled. "I guess you could say your son has followed in your footsteps."

Mr. Simpson winked. "Pamela was always getting into one jam or another when we were courting. I went along with her because I really did admire her stuff, and" — he smiled — "it was a bit of a lark. Especially that incident where she thought her new neighbour was a spy for the Soviet Union."

"I think I've heard that sort of thing before," Brisbois murmured.

"I think the outfits Mrs. Rudley chose from Riverboat are charming," Tiffany said. She stood on tiptoe to see over the crowd. The reception was in full swing, guests sitting here and there on lawn chairs, wandering from group to group, balancing plates of salmon and asparagus quiche, glasses of wine and iced tea. "When will the bride be throwing the bouquet?"

"I don't know," said Tim. "But I think I'll be making myself scarce for that, thank you." He plucked an olive from a condiment tray. "That thing has pieces of driftwood and shells in it, and some kind of bramble."

Gregoire cast a look of satisfaction toward the buffet. "She made it herself, which makes it unique and special." He checked his watch. "In a few minutes I should be bringing down the desserts."

Tiffany clapped her hands. "And the cake."

"The cake," said Gregoire, "will not be coming out until I have the undivided attention of the blessed couple."

Tiffany scanned the crowd. "Mr. Simpson is just over there with the Benson sisters, but I don't see Miss Miller." She smiled. "Oh, there she is, talking to Herb." She lowered her voice. "Aunt Pearl's taken quite a shine to him."

"When he is fixed up, he is actually quite an attractive man," said Gregoire. "Almost distinguished."

Tiffany nodded. "Perhaps if he were to establish a permanent residence, he could collect his pension and have a reasonable life. I know the Rudleys would fix him a room in the coach house."

"I don't think he wants that," said Gregoire. "He is footloose and fancy-free. The world is his oyster."

"I'll bet that oyster gets chilly around January," said Tim. He glanced around. "I don't think the romance of the wedding rubbed off on the Lawrences. She's standing by herself, looking down in the mouth. He's glad-handing with the rest of the guests."

"I am so looking forward to the bride throwing the bouquet," Tiffany said. She edged away, ignoring Officer Owens, who was waving at her hopefully.

"Tiffany is determined to catch the bouquet," Tim said. "I don't know why. It's not as if things are going smoothly with any of her beaux."

Gregoire aimed an index finger at him. "You do not understand the mystique surrounding the catching of the bouquet. It singles you out to all of the eligible bachelors."

"I didn't know you were such an expert on bouquets."

"I have caught one or two, although it was by accident." Gregoire straightened his tie. "I'm going up for the desserts."

Elizabeth Miller thought she had lost sight of her quarry. She had watched during the ceremony as Bonnie crept closer to Herb, hovering like a moth before a flame. She had headed in her direction but was detained by groups of well-wishers. She had to stop and acknowledge them and thank them for attending, a sentiment she felt sincerely but found inconvenient at that moment. By the time she reached Herb, she had lost sight of Bonnie. She chatted with Herb for a few minutes, then began to work her way through the crowd again. Finally, she reached clear ground. She hoisted up her skirts, climbed up onto a bench, and caught sight of Bonnie working her way toward the edge of the crowd, a frozen smile on her face, a hurried word here and there. She reached the edge of the crowd, took a quick look back, then scurried away.

Elizabeth looked around. Where was Detective Brisbois? She scanned the crowd but couldn't spot Creighton, who should have towered over everyone. Edward was halfway across the lawn in conversation with Mr. Bole. She hesitated, then made a decision. She hopped off the bench and headed toward the cabins, nodding and smiling to the Sawchucks, who assumed she was headed for a bathroom and made no attempt to detain her. She skipped past the inn and down past the Elm Pavilion.

Bonnie entered her cabin. Elizabeth crouched behind a spruce and waited.

Within minutes, Bonnie Lawrence reappeared, something balled up in her fist. She cast a frightened look around, then headed toward a garbage can at the back of the Elm Pavilion. She lifted the lid, dithered, then turned away and headed back toward her cottage. She stopped at the doorway, vacillated, then headed west along the lake and into the woods. Elizabeth Miller stepped out from behind the tree and followed, darting in and out among the trees. Bonnie stopped at a bluff fifteen feet above the water.

Elizabeth stepped forward. "Bonnie."

Bonnie Lawrence turned, her face frozen in horror. Then she smiled. "Why, Elizabeth, you startled me."

"What are you doing?"

Bonnie fisted her hands at her sides. "I wanted to get away for a few minutes. Weddings are so intense."

Elizabeth took a step forward. "What do you have in your hand?"

Bonnie laughed. "Oh, just something I picked up." She shrugged helplessly. "This is so embarrassing. It's a secret. A little tradition of mine. When I attend a wedding on the water, I like to throw something out onto the waves. It's good luck." She turned toward the lake.

Before Elizabeth could react, Bonnie tossed the object toward the lake. "There," she said, smiling, "done."

Elizabeth ran to the bank and looked down. The object Bonnie had thrown had missed. It lay a foot from the water's edge, riding back and forth on the ebb and flow.

The next thing Elizabeth Miller knew, she was tumbling down the embankment.

"Miss Miller." Gregoire broke through the foliage, stopped, his jaw dropping as he saw Bonnie push Miss Miller. "My God."

Bonnie hurtled past him toward the cabins.

Gregoire ran to the edge of the bluff. "Miss Miller."

She lay there, face down in the water.

"Miss Miller." He scrambled down the bank, reached Miss Miller, and pulled her out of the water. "Are you all right?"

Chapter 19

Elizabeth Miller lay on the settee on the veranda while the paramedics flashed lights in her eyes and questioned her about the date and her whereabouts. Simpson hovered at the railing.

The paramedic inspected the wound. "Superficial," she said. She took out a large Band-Aid.

"Lucky that drop wasn't any further," said Brisbios.

"Lucky Gregoire was so eager for you to see the cake," said Tim.

Brisbois pushed his hat back. "Gregoire saved the day. If he hadn't pulled you out right away, you would have drowned." He stood up. "Are you guys going to take her in?"

"To be on the safe side," said the paramedic over Miss Miller's protests.

Brisbois held up a hand. "Do what she says, Miss Miller."

"But I want to know what happens."

He grinned. "I'll talk to you afterwards. Right now, I've got some work to do."

Bonnie Lawrence looked very small, sitting in the chair across the table, her arms wrapped around her chest. She had been fingerprinted and photographed, not looking her best, hair dishevelled, eyes wide and unblinking.

"Bonnie," said Brisbois, "we're going to be taping this interview. You understand?"

She nodded.

"You need to answer in words."

"Yes," she said.

Brisbois read the particulars into the record, noting the presence of Bonnie's lawyer, a tired-looking man from a prestigious firm. The lawyer had rushed down from Ottawa the minute he received the call.

Brisbois had Bonnie state her name and address, then sat back to review his notes. Creighton sat beside him, his legs crossed.

Brisbois put his notes aside and leaned forward. "Mrs. Lawrence, you understand why you're here?"

She smiled like an eager student about to give a correct answer. "Because I killed Evelyn Hopper, and you think I tried to kill Miss Miller."

Brisbois nodded. "A witness, Mr. Gregoire Rochon, saw you push Elizabeth Miller off the bluff. She fell fifteen feet into the water. She was knocked unconscious. If Mr. Rochon hadn't come along, she would have drowned."

"I suppose so." Bonnie sighed, then brightened. "But I had to."

"You had to?"

"Yes. She recognized my scarf. The hobo must have found it. He was wearing it." She shuddered. "I know I'll never be able to wear it again, not after he's had it around his neck."

Brisbois stared at her.

The lawyer touched her arm. "Bonnie."

She pushed his hand away. "It matches Tee's tie. I knew she'd noticed that. I had to get rid of it." She wrung her hands. "I didn't know what else to do."

"Let me repeat for the record," — Brisbois glanced at his notes — "you've previously confessed to killing Evelyn Hopper and have signed a document to that effect."

She hesitated. "Yes."

"And in that confession you said you pushed Elizabeth Miller because you were worried about the scarf. You knew you had lost it in the woods the night you assaulted Evelyn Hopper. You've admitted you assaulted Elizabeth Miller because you believed she recognized the scarf and deduced you had killed Mrs. Hopper." He shrugged. "You were correct. That's exactly what Elizabeth Miller deduced."

"Yes." Bonnie shook her head slightly. "I know. I could see her even during the ceremony. She was looking around. She wasn't behaving like any other bride I've ever seen. I had to get away. I knew she was looking at me and at the hobo. I knew she knew the scarf was a match for Tee's tie and she knew what had happened. I had to get rid of the tie." She glanced at her lawyer. He was busy taking notes. "Miss Miller is one of those women who couldn't imagine coordinating her accessories with her husband's. She never said that directly, but she said other things. I knew what she was thinking. Everybody else always said how nice we looked together."

Brisbois smiled. "You did."

"And if she'd just minded her own business…" Bonnie stopped, flushed, apparently aware of the anger in her voice.

Brisbois waited her out. When she spoke again her voice had recaptured its sweet, pleading tone.

"She followed me. What was I supposed to do ?" Bonnie looked to Brisbois for validation, got a blank stare. Creighton answered her by looking away.

Brisbois looked down at his notes. "Now, reading from your previous statement, on the night Evelyn Hopper was killed, you went to her home. You wanted to talk to her because you thought she and your husband were having an affair."

The expression in her eyes sharpened. "I know they were. I followed them in the city. Tee and I used to have lunch together every day. Then he started making excuses. It was her. He was seeing her."

"Did you confront him about the affair?"

She studied her hands. "No," she said finally. "I thought he would get tired of her. I thought if I didn't let on I knew, we could just go on as if nothing had happened. But when he said he wanted to come here for his fishing trip — he takes one every year — I knew he was coming to see her."

"So you decided to come too."

Judith Alguire

She leaned forward. "Yes. I knew he was surprised. I never want to go on his fishing trips. He tried to talk me out of it. He said I'd be bored. I told him I'd seen a brochure for the Pleasant, about all the wonderful art colonies nearby, the boutiques. He usually goes places you have to fly in by float plane. So I knew it was her. I thought if I was with him I wouldn't have to worry." She paused. "Then he signed up for the night fishing trip. I knew he was trying to get away to see her." She laughed. "I didn't know what to do."

"Why didn't you go with him?"

She looked at him, repulsed. "I hate fishing. Tee knows I hate fishing."

"So what did you do?"

"I thought he'd probably planned to go to her house. So I waited until after dinner. Everybody was busy up at the inn. I thought nobody would see me. I walked up the side road. It wasn't very far."

"You walked up the side road to Mrs. Hopper's home."

"Yes."

"What happened next?"

"There was nobody there," she said. "Her car was gone. There were no lights on in the house. I waited. Then I decided she and Tee had planned to meet somewhere else." She swallowed hard. "Maybe in a motel or something. I was just about to leave when I saw the headlights of a car pulling into the laneway."

"Then what?"

"She went into the house. I didn't know what to do. I hid beside the house. I almost went back to the Pleasant but, then, just as I was going to do that, she came out. I introduced myself. I said I wanted to talk to her about Tee." Her voice shook. "She just gave me this look. As if I was nothing. She brushed past me and went on down to the stable." She stopped, struggling to control her voice.

Brisbois gave her a minute to compose herself. "Please continue, Mrs. Lawrence. Tell us what happened next."

Bonnie took a deep breath. "I followed her. She was saddling the horse. I tried to talk to her. She laughed at me again. She told me I was stupid, that Tee was tired of me and was going to leave me." She dabbed at her eyes. "I couldn't bear hearing her say that. She got up on the horse. I didn't intend to hurt her. I was just trying to talk to her. I begged her to stay away from Tee. She gave me this smile. It was so condescending. She was so cold. There was a shovel. I grabbed it. I just wanted to get her attention. I wanted her to take me seriously. I didn't hit her that hard, but the horse reared up. She didn't fall off but she couldn't control it. It ran off."

Brisbois waited.

"I didn't know what to do. I just wanted to get away from there. But I had to talk to her, to tell her I didn't mean to hurt her. I didn't want her to tell Tee what I did. I thought if I offered her some money. Most people…" She paused, then said in a whisper, "Most people like money."

"What did you do next?"

"I followed her." She sighed. "It was terrible. I kept catching my clothes on the trees. My clothes were ruined."

Creighton disguised a derisive grunt with a cough. Brisbois gave him a sharp look, then turned back to Bonnie. "Please, continue."

"I found her. She was lying on the ground."

"Dead?"

"I don't know. I said her name, but she didn't answer."

"So you bashed her head in to make sure," Brisbois said casually.

She looked at him bewildered. "No."

He reviewed his notes, said without looking up, "Come on, Bonnie, half of her skull was missing."

Her voice rose in dismay. "No, that's not true. I couldn't have. I wasn't close enough. I was afraid of the horse. It was standing right beside her."

Brisbois reached for an envelope. "I can show you the pictures, Bonnie. Her skull's bashed in."

She stared at the envelope, brow furrowed. "She fell off the horse and hit her head on a rock. Somebody at the inn said that."

"But you must have seen that when you saw her lying there on the ground. That she had this big dent in the back of her head, blood running down onto her shirt."

"No," she protested. "I told you, I wasn't that close to her."

He put the envelope aside. "Her head was bashed in, Bonnie, and it wasn't the result of her falling from the horse."

She didn't respond.

"So you went back to the inn," he said.

"Yes," she said, subdued.

"Which way did you go?"

She looked up, confused. "I went back the way I came. On the side road. I didn't know how to get there through the woods. I didn't know it was so close."

"What time did you get back?"

"About ten-thirty, I think."

"And you told everybody you'd spent the whole evening in your cabin going through wedding magazines."

"Yes."

"Did you ever think of calling an ambulance for Mrs. Hopper? In case she wasn't dead?"

She looked at him, round-eyed. "I couldn't do that. Then everybody would have known." She wrung her hands. "I did do something."

"What did you do?"

"When Tee came home, I told him."

"And what was his reaction?"

"He told me she was lying. He said he knew her but just because he'd met her at a convention, that she'd wormed her way into some meetings with him. She wanted to get a contract to redecorate his offices." She looked at him, defiant. "You have to see it was her fault. She was forcing herself on Tee."

Brisbois considered this. "You know, Bonnie, men don't usually have trouble fending off these sorts of advances." He paused. "If they want to." She opened her mouth to protest. He stopped her with a question. "So you told Tee. He denied having a relationship with Evelyn Hopper. Then what?"

Her gaze drifted to the wall over his shoulder. "He asked me if I was sure she was dead. I said I wasn't. Not a hundred per cent. He said he'd have to check because, if she was still alive, we would have to call an ambulance. I didn't want him to go, but he insisted. He waited until the lights in the other cabins were out, then he went up there. When he came back he said she was dead. We put our clothes and shoes into a garbage bag. Tee pretended he was going fishing the next morning. He took the bag and dropped it in the lake by those shoal markers."

"So Tee was involved."

She looked at him, smiled. "All he did was get rid of the clothes. He didn't do anything wrong. He did it for me. Because I'm his wife and he loves me. Wouldn't you do that for your wife?"

He didn't answer. He knew in his heart he'd break every law on the books to protect Mary, especially if, like Tee, it was his behaviour that had set the tragedy in motion.

"So," he said finally, "you thought you were home free and then you started to worry that Elizabeth Miller knew too much."

She nodded. "I'd heard others — the staff, some of the guests — talking about how smart she was, about how she had helped solve crimes before. Tim, the waiter, said she'd have this one solved before the police."

Brisbois kept his expression neutral.

"Then, at the wedding, I saw her looking at that hobo and at me. Right in the middle of the ceremony. She couldn't keep her eyes off us. I knew then that she knew." She looked down at the table, defeated, then said quietly, "I suppose I panicked. But I couldn't keep pretending. It was too much. Trying to hold things together, trying to act as if nothing had happened. I'd been doing it so long. Mrs. Hopper, then that awful Mr. Arnold."

Brisbois straightened. The lawyer shook his head, puzzled.

She shivered. "He was watching me all the time. At first I thought he was just being flirtatious. Then he told me he had seen me going up the side road that night, when I'd told everybody I hadn't left my cabin. He said if I paid him fifty-thousand dollars, he'd forget he saw me."

The lawyer put up a hand. "One moment. I want to confer with my client."

Bonnie shook him off. "No, I want to explain."

"I must advise you…"

She turned to him, eyes blazing. "I'm tired of all this. Besides, when you hear…"

Brisbois sat back. "How did it happen, Bonnie?"

She paused to compose herself, looked him straight in the eye. "We agreed to meet the night of the bridge tournament. I pretended I didn't know Blackwood's convention." She smiled. "That was hard, after all the afternoons I've played bridge. I made sure we lost the hand so I could excuse myself. I knew Norman was glad to see me go. I slipped out and went to Mr. Arnold's cabin. Everybody was so busy they didn't notice me leaving. Even Tee didn't notice." She pressed her lips together for a few moments, then continued. "I had some Benadryl capsules. I'd taken them apart and emptied the powder into my compact. I knew he used Benadryl. I heard that boy tell him he shouldn't, that he shouldn't mix it with alcohol."

"What did you do with the capsules?"

"I flushed them down the toilet."

"What about the blister packs?"

"I cut them into little pieces and flushed them, the package too." Brisbois nodded. "Go on."

"I went to his cabin. He had been drinking. A lot, I think. He always drank a lot. I told him I would write him a cheque. He laughed and said maybe I could throw in something extra. He touched me." She shuddered. "I played along. I told him I'd need a drink. He poured the drink. I said I needed ginger ale. While he went to get it, I put the Benadryl in his drink."

"And he didn't notice?"

"No. I distracted him. I got him talking about how we would launder the money."

"So he could account for the sudden jump in his bank account."

"Yes. I told him we would write up an agreement for some work at the cottage. I wrote the cheque."

He nodded. "Please continue."

"He finished that drink and had two more. I said I was ready but that I had to go to the bathroom. I waited." She took a deep breath. "I was so frightened. I thought he might come and drag me out. After a while, I didn't hear him moving around, so I came out. He had passed out on the bed."

"Was he dead when you left?"

"He had passed out," she repeated. She paused, a look of revulsion crossing her face. "Then he started to vomit." She put a hand to her mouth. "I never could stand to see anyone vomit. I took the cheque and left. I just prayed."

"That he wouldn't make it."

Her jaw trembled. "I felt so relieved when I heard he was dead. I know that was wrong. But after what he tried to do, he deserved what happened."

"What did you tell Tee?"

"I didn't tell Tee." She leaned forward, gave him a desperate look. "Detective, you have to understand. I did this for us. I did it for Tee. Everybody wanted him to run in the next election. He would have won." She stopped. "Maybe he still can. Someday, when people forget."

Bonnie had been taken away. Brisbois sat, staring at his notes. "Do you think people will forget?" Creighton asked. "Make Tee our next prime minister?"

Brisbois snorted. "Sure, give them a year or so. The public has the attention span of a snail."

"I'll bet that lawyer's already started working on the insanity defence."

"He just might be successful with that," Brisbois murmured.

"Do you think she's insane?"

Brisbois thought about that. "I think she has a one-track mind and a skewed sense of morality."

"I don't think that counts as insanity. I think that's what they call a character flaw."

Brisbois smiled. "You really got into that course, didn't you?" He was quiet for a few moments, then said, "Just between the two of us, I think Bonnie Lawrence is as crazy as a loon."

"When are we going to see Tee?"

Brisbois closed his notebook. "I think we'll let him stew a bit. It'll pump up his imagination."

"He'll probably start making noise if we don't let him see Bonnie soon. He's probably been tying himself in knots, wondering what she's been saying."

Brisbois smiled. "I'll bet he has. We've got to stall him long enough to get a report from the dive team." He paused, opened his notebook. "Who went out with them?"

"Maroni and Petrie."

"Good."

Creighton stretched, yawned. "I suppose if they don't come up with the goods before Tee blows his stack, we could wing it."

Brisbois smiled. "We could and we could make ourselves" — he hooked his fingers in quotation marks — "unavailable."

"Could we grab a bite while we're being unavailable?"

Brisbois looked at him in mock surprise. "You know, I think we could."

Chapter 20

A subdued Tee Lawrence sat in the interview room.

"Bonnie told me what she'd done," he said. He stared at the table. "When I got home, she was just sitting there in the dark. I know I should have contacted the police. You have to understand, I was trying to protect my wife."

Brisbois nodded. "Of course. Tell us what happened, Mr. Lawrence."

Tee moistened his lips. "After Bonnie told me what had happened, I went up into the woods. I was hoping" — he shook his head — "praying that Mrs. Hopper was still alive."

Brisbois made a note. "So you just went up through the woods?"

Tee shook his head. "No, I went around on the side road. I knew the Rudleys were camping out back of the inn. Everybody had been talking about that."

"So you took the road. Did you drive? Walk?"

"I walked." Tee paused, his jaw muscles bunching. "Every step, I was afraid of running into somebody coming home late. It was unnerving."

"Where was Mrs. Hopper when you found her?"

He gulped, took a moment to respond. "She was lying on the ground, face down. The horse was beside her. I guess I spooked him. He bolted when I approached her."

"And what about Mrs. Hopper?"

Tee shook his head. "She was dead. I couldn't do anything. I went back to the cottage. I told Bonnie."

"How did she take the news? That Mrs. Hopper was dead?"

Tee gave him a look of incredulity. "She was distraught." He took a deep breath. "I told her I'd do whatever I could to protect her. I put our clothes in a garbage bag and dumped the bag in the lake the next morning."

Brisbois paused. "Yes, Mrs. Lawrence told us." He smiled. "And we found it." He sat back in his chair. "You were smart to drop it by the shoal markers in one way, Mr. Lawrence. People tend to avoid shoal markers. On the other hand, those areas usually have rocks, some of them hidden. The bag ended up on a shelf about six feet down. It wasn't hard to find. As I said, it wasn't far down. And it was orange. It stuck out like a sore thumb. Our dive team barely had to get their flippers wet."

Tee looked hurt. "I'm not a seasoned criminal. I was just trying to help out my wife."

Brisbois pretended not to have heard. He flipped through his notes, stopped. "OK, up in the woods." He looked at Tee. "Know what we found?"

Tee looked annoyed. "No, Detective, I don't."

"We found a gold star, you know the kind grade-school teachers hand out."

"OK."

"The night you went out on the charter, you got the gold star. You got all the gold stars because every fish you caught was bigger than anything anybody else caught."

Tee shrugged. "That's right."

Brisbois smiled. "Congratulations. So" — he continued — "what did you do with all your gold stars? Did you stick them on your pole, the way you're supposed to on Doretta's boat?"

Tee gave him a sheepish smile. "No, I threw them away as soon as I got off the boat. I didn't want them on my pole but I didn't want to hurt the lady's feelings."

Brisbois nodded. "That was thoughtful." He waited a moment. "Would it surprise you to know we found one of those stars up in the woods near Mrs. Hopper's body?"

Tee sighed. "No, it wouldn't, Detective. I was up in the woods. I told you that. I suppose one of the stars stuck to my clothing and fell off later."

"Hm." Brisbois flipped through his notes, turned to Creighton, whispered behind his hand.

Creighton took out his notes, checked them, nodded.

Brisbois turned his attention back to Tee. "The shoes we found in the garbage bag, were those the ones you wore on the boat?"

"Yes."

"Our people lifted part of a footprint near Mrs. Hopper's body, not much but very well-preserved. It matched the tread and markings on your shoe."

Tee shook his head. "Detective, I don't see the point of this. I've already told you I was in the woods."

Brisbois regarded him evenly. "Yes, you did." He returned to his notebook.

Tee broke the silence. "Look, I know I'm in trouble here — getting rid of evidence, not reporting a crime — but I was trying to protect my wife."

"Maybe you should have thought of that before you hooked up with Evelyn Hopper," Brisbois said without looking up.

Tee uttered an impatient sigh. "I wasn't having an affair with Evelyn Hopper."

Brisbois looked up. "You weren't?"

Tee gave him a weary smile. "I met Evelyn a few times for lunch. I was thinking of having our offices redecorated."

"Why would your wife think you were having an affair?"

Tee shook his head. "You want the whole story?"

Brisbois nodded. "That would be refreshing."

Tee ran a hand through his hair. "I hate to say what I'm about to say. I feel as if I'm betraying Bonnie, making her look weak, foolish."

"We already know she's a murderer, Mr. Lawrence. I don't think it can get too much worse."

"OK." Tee took a deep breath. "You have to understand, Detective, Bonnie is pretty insecure. She doesn't have much education. I met her when she was working as a hostess at a boat show one summer. She had the right manners, knew how to dress. She presented well. Still, she had some trouble fitting in. She didn't have the background. Then she started helping people out with weddings. She got a lot of accolades for that. It became her thing." He paused, coughed. "I'm afraid I didn't take that talent too seriously. I was pretty insensitive about it, as a matter of fact. She wanted children. She was told she couldn't have them. We could have adopted, but I think she saw that as another failure. She got more insecure after that. If I didn't return her calls right away, if I had to cancel a lunch date, if I was a few minutes late coming home from work, she assumed I was seeing someone. I didn't pick up on how serious the situation was. I was working."

"You were working."

Tee bit his lower lip. "I'm not proud of my behaviour, Detective. I should have taken some time off, taken her on one of those romantic Caribbean vacations — she would have liked that — done something to make her feel special."

"Instead, you brought her to an inn, a half-mile away from the woman she thought you were having the affair with."

Tee spread his arms. "Detective, when I booked the trip, I didn't know she thought we were having an affair. I had mentioned to Evelyn that I was looking for something different for my annual fishing trip. She suggested the Pleasant. I didn't know Bonnie thought we were having an affair until that night. I screwed up, but I can't do anything about it now." He slumped back in his chair. "I had to stand by Bonnie. She would have been devastated if I'd called the police."

Brisbois watched him for a moment "How far were you prepared to go to cover up for your wife?"

"As far as I had to."

"Including covering up the fact that she murdered Jack Arnold?"

"What?"

"Your wife has confessed to helping him along with a spiked drink."

Tee's face collapsed. "I didn't know. I didn't know. My God, she must have had a complete breakdown."

Brisbois tapped his pen against his notebook. "It's too bad Bonnie thought she had to deal with Mr. Arnold. She said he was trying to blackmail her. He told her he saw her going up the side road the night Evelyn Hopper was murdered. Bonnie told everybody she'd never left her cabin."

Tee shook his head.

"If she hadn't killed Arnold," Brisbois continued, "she might have had a future to look forward to. She might have got a break for Evelyn's murder. Maybe manslaughter. But what happened to Mr. Arnold, that was planned. And that means murder, Mr. Lawrence."

Tee stared at the table.

Brisbois turned to Creighton. "Have you got those photographs? And can you tell us what that report says?"

"The report says Mrs. Hopper's tissue and blood were found on a rock at the scene," Creighton said. He handed the photographs to Brisbois.

Brisbois turned to Tee. "What do you think about that?"

Tee moistened his lips. "I don't know."

Brisbois held up the first photograph. "This is the rock."

Tee stared at the photograph. "All right."

"You remember that we found your footprints up there."

Tee's gaze wandered. "We've already talked about that. I said…"

Brisbois interrupted. "We agreed the print matched the tread and markings on the shoe you were wearing that night."

Tee sighed. "I don't know what you're getting at, Detective. I was in the woods. I was near Evelyn's body. I left footprints. So what?"

Brisbois pulled out the second photograph. "We found the footprint under the rock." He smiled. "How do you suppose it got there, Mr. Lawrence?"

Chapter 21

Detective Brisbois faced Elizabeth Miller over the table in the dining room at the Pleasant. "I'm glad I caught you before you left. I wanted a chance to wish you well."

"Why, thank you, Detective."

"I hear you're headed to Algonquin Park."

"I want to show Edward the real wilderness."

"I hope you're taking plenty of bug spray."

"A Girl Scout is always prepared."

He didn't respond for a moment, just stirred his coffee, enjoying the quiet of the dining room after the breakfast rush. "You have a good eye, Miss Miller. That scarf didn't look like much when we packed up Herb's things."

"We can thank Mrs. Rudley for cleaning it up."

He nodded. "And for so much more." He paused. "Still, if Bonnie hadn't panicked, we might not have been able to get her on the scarf alone. If she'd had the presence of mind, she could have said she dropped the scarf anywhere around the place and Herb picked it up." He shrugged. "I hate to say this, but she isn't the sharpest knife in the drawer."

"She lost her nerve."

"Yes, the stress of trying to hold things together got to her, for sure. When she saw you looking at the scarf, it was almost a signal for her to let go."

"I could forgive Bonnie," Elizabeth said. "Everything she thought was important in her life was in danger of being taken away—first by Evelyn Hopper, then by Jack Arnold. But what Tee tried to do is unforgivable."

He nodded. "Evelyn was still alive when he found her. At that point he could have saved Evelyn and saved Bonnie. If Evelyn had survived, Bonnie would have had a chance to reclaim her life."

"It was all about him."

"He was ambitious," Brisbois said. "He thought, if he killed Evelyn, he would be free to pursue a political career. He figured, in the worst-case scenario, if Bonnie got caught, he could at least go on as before. But if Evelyn lived, the story of his infidelity would come out."

Elizabeth gave him a chagrinned smile. "He thought his career could withstand his wife's criminality better than his infidelity."

"Yes. Hard to understand."

She looked pensive, sat stirring her coffee lazily.

"A penny for your thoughts," said Brisbois.

"Maybe implicating Tee was Bonnie's ultimate revenge. She didn't have to say he was involved in anything. After all, she didn't know he had killed Evelyn."

Brisbois raised his brows. "You mean maybe she wasn't as dumb as she seemed?"

Elizabeth smiled. "At least, now, she knows exactly where he is at every minute. Probably for the first time in years."

"I hope we never see him again, Margaret," Rudley said as Brisbois disappeared down the front steps.

"Be nice, Rudley."

"If he insists upon coming here for dinner, we won't stop him, of course. But I'll be damned if he's going to make a career of this place." He looked up as Lloyd entered the lobby.

"There's a man out there who wants to talk to you," said Lloyd, motioning toward the veranda.

"Did he say what it was about?"

"Just that he had to talk to Mr. Rudley."

"Probably some damned salesman," Rudley muttered. He charged out onto the veranda.

A few minutes later, he returned.

"What was that about, Rudley?"

"That was the Reverend McBroom from St. Peter's in Brockton."

She frowned. "Where are your manners? You should have invited him in for tea."

"He heard about the wedding." He slipped in behind the desk, stood, fiddling with the register.

"Out with it, Rudley."

"Very well." He paused, gathering his thoughts. "It seems, Margaret, that the Reverend Pendergast was involved in an incident at St. Peter's Parish Hall recently."

Her brow furrowed.

"It seems that while a guest at the one-hundredth anniversary of the St. Peter's Ladies' Auxiliary, while tea was being served, the Reverend Pendergast proposed a toast, then, to everyone's consternation, he dropped his pants."

She put a hand to her mouth. "I trust he was wearing underwear."

"Not a stitch."

"Oh, dear."

"So," Rudley continued, "the bishop called the reverend in to account for his behaviour. He found him a tad senile. He decided to keep the matter under wraps — well, as much as you can keep anything under wraps when it's done in front of fifty old ladies — and allow him to enjoy an honourable retirement. Part of the understanding was that the old pisspot would refrain from performing the sacraments."

She looked at him in horror. "Do you mean they're not married?"

"Quite right. But no matter. Reverend McBroom will contact the young couple and sanctify their vows in some sort of backroom ceremony."

"They're headed into the wilderness without benefit of clergy."

He put an arm around her. "No matter, Margaret. It's not as if they haven't been there before."

About the Author

Judith Alguire's previous novels include *Pleasantly Dead* and *The Pumpkin Murders*, the first two books of the Rudley Mysteries, as well as *All Out* and *Iced*, both of which explored the complex relationships of sportswomen on and off the playing field. Her short stories, articles and essays have also appeared in such publications as *The Malahat Review* and *Harrowsmith*, and she is a past member of the editorial board of the *Kingston Whig-Standard*. A graduate of Queen's University, she has recently retired from nursing.

"Alguire is clearly of the sly and cosy old-school British detective fiction à la Agatha Christie's Miss Marple. And that's a venerable genre of mystery writing." —*Winnipeg Free Press*

"If a British-style 'cosy' mystery usually resembles a stroll through the dark side of a park, *The Pumpkin Murders* is a 100-yard dash — with attitude. Autumn in Ontario cottage country: scarlet colours, crisp evenings and morning frost — with a female impersonator on the run and some very annoyed drug dealers. More than just pumpkins get smashed at Pleasant Inn this Halloween. The same group of characters from Alguire's first mystery is back, including the owners of Pleasant Inn, cops whose whistles are short of a full blast, vintage card-sharp aunties and murder victims. Snappish dialogue fuels the pace with good one-liners spicing up the tone and revealing a variety of gaudy characters and quaint settings. *The Pumpkin Murders* is a cheery resurgence of the British standby — in Canadian style."

—Don Graves, *The Hamilton Spectator*

ISBN 978-18987109-37-3

Also available as an eBook
ISBN 978-18987109-68-7

Trevor and Margaret Rudley have had their share of misfortunes at
The Pleasant Inn, the cherished Ontario cottage-country hotel they've
owned for twenty-five years. There have been boating accidents,
accidental poisonings, and then there was that unfortunate ski-lift
incident. But this year their hopes are high for the summer season.
However, barely a week goes by and their hopes dashed. There's
a dead body making a nuisance of itself in the wine cellar, and it's
nobody the Rudleys know.

The guests at The Pleasant Inn, a wealthy and eccentric lot,
are dying for distraction, and one of them, Miss Miller, sets out to
solve the case of the deceased, relying on wild speculation, huge leaps
of logic, and the assistance of her great admirer, Edward Simpson,
who is too smitten to dissuade her from her adventure in detection.
Challenging her in the race to resolution is the disciplined Detective
Brisbois, whose deep-rooted insecurities about his style and status are
aroused by the hotel guests' careless assumption of privilege. When
Brisbois stumbles into peril of his own, the intrepid Miss Miller is the
only one left who can solve the crime.

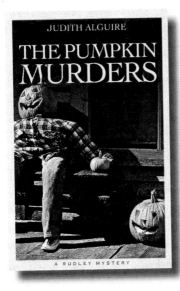

ISBN 978-18987109-45-8

Also available as an eBook
ISBN 978-18987109-69-4

Autumn returns to Ontario cottage country. Leaves redden. Pumpkins ripen. And Trevor and Margaret Rudley, proprietors of the Pleasant Inn, expect nothing more than a little Halloween high jinks to punctuate the mellow ambiance of their much-loved hostelry. However, the frost is barely on the pumpkin when Gerald, an old female-impersonator friend of the Pleasant's esteemed cook Gregoire, turns up, dragging his very frightened friend Adolph behind. They've witnessed a drug deal in progress in Montreal and they're on the lam, hoping to blend into the Pleasant's pleasant rhythms until the heat is off. Alas, they hope in vain.

As the bodies pile up, the intrepid Elizabeth Miller jumps into the fray, fully armed with her peculiar intuition, her maddening charm, and her devoted swain, Edward Simpson, who proves a useful fellow behind the wheel of a car. Detective Michel Brisbois, in the past bested by Miss Miller in rooting out unpleasantness at the Pleasant, finds himself racing — quite literally — to keep up with his amateur challenger. But when the chips are down — as they inevitably are — it's the laziest creature on earth who ends up saving the day for the kindly and rather eccentric folk of Ontario's most peculiar country hotel.